The Dead Who Love

By Jennifer St. Clair

Writers Exchange E-Publishing
http://www.writers-exchange.com

The Dead Who Do Not Sleep
Copyright 2004, 2015, 2023 Jennifer St. Clair
Writers Exchange E-Publishing
PO Box 372
ATHERTON QLD 4883

Cover Art by: Jatin

Published by Writers Exchange E-Publishing
http://www.writers-exchange.com

The unauthorized reproduction or distribution of this copyrighted work is illegal. Criminal copyright infringement, including infringement without monetary gain, is investigated by the FBI and is punishable by up to 5 (five) years in federal prison and a fine of $250,000.

Names, characters and incidents depicted in this book are products of the author's imagination and are used fictitiously. Any resemblance to actual events, locales, organizations, or persons, living or dead, is entirely coincidental and beyond the intent of the author.

No part of this book may be reproduced or transmitted in any form or any means, electronic or mechanical, including photocopying, recording, or by any information storage and retrieval system, without permission from the publisher.

Dedication

To Mom and Dad, because you deserve to have one of your own.

Chapter 1

The pounding on my door jerked me out of sleep like a cold shower, dousing the fire of my dreams with stark reality. I cracked open one eye and stared at the clock. *Three a.m.? Who would be pounding on my door at three a.m.? Was the apartment building on fire?*

I rolled out of bed, staggered for a bit until I found my balance, and pulled on a pair of dirty shorts. The kitchen light sent shards of agony deep inside my brain when I flicked it on. I squinted, my eyes watering, and fumbled with the lock.

Two men in dark, double-breasted suits stood in the hallway, their hands clasped behind their backs. I stepped back involuntarily, raising my hand above my eyes to I block the glare of the light, but it didn't help. I had never seen them before in my life.

"Will Spark?"

The taller one had a nasal Brooklyn accent that grated across my nerves and sent them singing. His nose skewed sideways, giving him the appearance of a wannabe prizefighter. His hair reminded me of a skunk, black as night and liberally shot with gray. The other man stroked a pencil thin blond moustache and gave me a smile that showed only a few of his crooked teeth.

"Yes?" I realized that was a mistake as soon as I said it; no one with legitimate concerns would pound on a guy's door at three in the morning.

They exchanged glances.

Brooklyn grinned at me, exposing capped white teeth. "May we come in?"

"I'm not sure..."

Before I could finish my refusal and shut the door in their faces, the blond one took me by one arm and propelled me backwards, into the kitchen. Brooklyn followed, still grinning.

"It will only take five minutes of your time, really," he said. "We only have a couple questions."

"Where is it?" the blond asked. He shook me and I felt another pang of agony shoot through my poor abused brain.

"Where is what?" I tried to pull away from him, but he was stronger than he looked. He calmly pulled me into the living room and pushed me into my favorite chair.

The first tendril of panic bloomed in my stomach. I tasted sour fear in the back of my throat. I tried to stand. The blond pushed me back down.

"Mr. William Spark." Brooklyn stood next to me, his arms folded against his chest. The guy had to be a bodybuilder or something; he outweighed and outmuscled me by at least a rottweiler. Whoever these guys were, they meant business, even though I had no idea what business they were in. Or what they wanted from me.

"Where is it?" the blond asked again.

"Tell us the truth, Will Spark," Brooklyn said, and pulled a switchblade from one of his pockets. He inspected his nails, and then methodically began to clean them with the tip of the blade. I couldn't tear my eyes away from it.

"Mr. Spark, we represent a certain...shall we say, party who is interested in something you saw right around midnight."

"Midnight?"

"Three hours and," he consulted a Rolex on his wrist, "four minutes ago."

"I was..." I trailed off when I realized I had no idea *where* I had been around midnight. "I was drunk." That much, at least, I remembered. I had gone to a party. Larry's party. And he had refused to give me back my keys. I had walked home in the dark, but I didn't remember one step of that journey.

"You weren't drunk enough," Brooklyn insisted. "Talk to us, Will Spark. What did you see and where did it go?"

"*It* what?" I shook my head, which only made things worse. "I don't know what you're talking about." I started to rise out of the chair, intending to lunge for the phone on the coffee table, and the blond punched me in the stomach.

I gagged and barely managed not to puke all over my nice clean carpet. Brooklyn grabbed a hunk of hair and pulled me up. The blond punched me again.

This time, I couldn't hold it back.

"Look at the mess you've made, Mr. Spark." The blond shook his head. Brooklyn handed me a handkerchief to wipe my mouth. He waited until I had straightened back up, and then he had the blond hit me again.

"Talk to us, Will Spark," Brooklyn said. "I *don't* want to have to hurt you."

"I don't want you to have to hurt me either," I gasped, struggling to catch my breath.

"Then tell us what you saw and where it went," the blond suggested.

"I don't know! I was drunk!" I didn't realize I was shouting until Brooklyn's hand covered my mouth.

"Quietly, Mr. Spark. We don't want to worry your neighbors."

I nodded, frantic to take a breath. When he removed his hand, I slumped in the chair and gasped for air.

"I was drunk," I finally said. "I don't remember much when I'm drunk."

"I think Mr. Spark needs some help with his memory, Lyle."

I tried to duck away from the blonde's punch, but I didn't duck fast enough. His fist slammed into the side of my head. I felt a burst of pure pain, and then nothing.

When I came to, I couldn't move. I raised my head and realized I sat in one of the old kitchen chairs I'd picked up at the local Goodwill, bound hand and foot with duct tape. I could move my hands in a limited way, but I could not escape. Duct tape isn't only good for pipes, after all.

Brooklyn and Lyle stood in front of the kitchen table, facing me. Lyle leaned against the battered table, his arms crossed. Brooklyn seemed bored, as if beating up a guy was all in a day's work. I had feeling it was, for them.

My head had stopped pounding. Now, it throbbed in time to my heartbeat, in great unending waves of pain. When I tried to focus on Brooklyn, the kitchen lurched around me head and I had to struggle not to gag.

"Should I hit him again, boss?" Lyle asked and raised one meaty fist.

Brooklyn stared at me for a moment. "Are you ready to talk to us, Will Spark?"

"I don't think I have anything to say," I whispered. My voice sounded funny and the whole left side of my face felt swollen and strange. I did not want to look in a mirror.

"What did you see and where did it go, Mr. Spark?" Brooklyn asked. "We wouldn't ask you if it wasn't important. It could be a matter of National Security."

"I doubt that," I muttered. Lyle raised his fist. I flinched back before I could stop myself.

Brooklyn smiled. "Hit him again, Lyle. See if you can jog his memory a bit."

"No, you don't have to hit..." my protest went unheard. Lyle drew his fist back and plunged it into my stomach. I tried to curl around the pain, but I couldn't move.

He hit me again for good measure, and I felt something pop inside my chest. Another streak of pain joined what already dimmed my fading vision. I tried to lose myself in darkness.

Brooklyn threw a cup of cold water in my face. It jerked me back to the present long enough for me to notice that the switchblade had reappeared. This time, Brooklyn wasn't cleaning his nails with it.

"I could kill you right now, Mr. Spark," he said, his voice both calm and cold. "I could drive this into your heart and you would die."

I stared at him. My stomach hurt too much to take a breath, let alone a deep one. "Why would you want to kill me?"

"You saw something you weren't supposed to see," Brooklyn said. "Lyle, I don't think hitting him will jog his memory. I think we'll have to do something a bit more...drastic."

"Drastic? Look, guys. I don't know who you are or who you work for, but could it be possible that you have the wrong..." I shut up when I saw the gun in Lyle's hand.

Brooklyn smiled. "*Now* we're beginning to understand each other. What did you see after you left the party, Mr. Spark?" He waved the knife in front of my face.

I tried to remember, I really did, but the whole previous evening was a smudge of booze in my memory. *Mom had been right. She'd always told me that drinking would bring me to a bad end.*

"Do you want me to shoot him now?" Lyle asked.

"Shoot me?" I tried to twist out of the chair, overbalanced, and ended up on my back, staring up at the fluorescents. I tasted blood in the back of my throat.

"Look, can't we talk about this?" I'd never been much of a fighter, but I didn't want to die.

Brooklyn bent over me. "We only came here to ask you a few questions, Mr. Spark. You refused to answer. What more can we do?"

"I don't remember!" I was babbling now, and we both knew it. "Hell, I'm lucky I remember where I live when I'm drunk. Ask any one of my friends. Ask my neighbors. Ask anyone you like, just don't..."

"I think it's too late," Lyle said, and leveled the gun at my head. I stared up at death. The words shriveled and died in my throat. A hot wetness spread over the crotch of my shorts.

Brooklyn turned away. "Lyle, you know what to do."

Lyle gave me a sorrowful look and pulled the trigger.

The gunshot deafened everything and sent me barreling down into darkness.

Chapter 2

When I opened my eyes, I found I sat on the top of a granite crypt in an unfamiliar cemetery. For a moment, the utter calmness of the place forestalled any questions I might have had, and I sat and enjoyed the spring sunshine for a little while until I realized something was not right.

I wore my favorite pair of jeans, and a black t-shirt with my oldest flannel shirt over it. My feet were bare, which wasn't that surprising; if I'd lived in the country instead of the city I probably would have gone barefoot most of the time. But they were clean, not dirty as if I had walked to this cemetery in a drunken stupor.

Had I been drinking last night? I tried to remember what had happened, but my memory would only give me glimpses of something I didn't really want to explore. I touched my ribs, expecting them to be broken, but they were unharmed. I touched my face. It seemed to be the same one I was used to, but I'd have to check a mirror to be sure of that.

Okay. I glanced around the cemetery. *First things first.* I'd find someone, figure out where I was and how I had come to be there, and then catch a cab home. I'd worry about the missing memories later. Maybe, just maybe, I'd cut down on the alcohol consumption for a bit. I hated waking up in strange places with no memory of how I had arrived.

The cemetery was awfully busy for an early morning. I wasn't used to getting up so early, but I had always assumed cemeteries to be quiet places, not the bustling metropolis I saw before me.

An old man and an even older lady played chess across a crypt a few feet away from me. Two little girls, one dressed in an odd frilly white dress with a huge bow in her hair and the other in more modern clothes played hide and seek among the gravestones to my right. A man in what looked to be a Civil War uniform lay under a low spreading tree to my left, his cap over his eyes. Straight in front of me, a large woman in a severe black sheath drawled on a cigarette holder that would have been perfect in *The Great Gatsby*. There were others wandering amid the gravestones as well, but I didn't pay much attention to them.

I drew my knees up to my chest and contemplated my surroundings. Something was wrong in the picture, but I couldn't quite pinpoint what the wrongness was. I stared at them, each in turn, and then realized they were not making any noise. The clicks of the chess pieces were the only things I could hear. Everything else--from the little girls' obvious laughter to the birds that should have been singing in the trees--had vanished as completely as my memory.

I looked at the old man and the shriveled old crone that was his companion. They seemed oblivious to me. I gripped the edge of the crypt, started to slide down to the ground, and realized I could see the grass right through my feet. Right *through* my feet.

Something dark broke loose in my mind. I felt a phantom pain shoot through my chest. I gasped, doubled over and slid the rest of the way to the ground. Cracking my head on the edge of the crypt should have hurt, but I didn't even feel the impact.

The old man said something to his companion and stood, pushing his lawn chair back against a gravestone. His companion giggled and glanced my way. She smiled at me, but I didn't have the strength to smile back.

Up close, the old man resembled my dead grandfather enough for me to instantly relax. He had weathered skin, and his blue eyes were almost lost in the web of wrinkles that surrounded them. He wore a pair of jeans as faded as mine and a blue button down shirt with the sleeves rolled up to his elbows. The patch above his breast read 'L. Perkins'. *His* feet weren't bare.

"Lysander Perkins." He held out his hand. I stared at it for a moment, and then shook. His grip was dry and firm, with no hint of weakness. "I expect you'll be having some questions?"

"Will Spark." I wet my lips and refused to look down at my feet. "Questions?"

Lysander hesitated. "You *do* know you're dead, right, son?"

"Dead?" I repeated. Something tried to tug loose in my mind, but I hastily shoved it away. "I can't be dead. I went to a party. I was...drunk." *But I had never woke up in a cemetery before...*

"Would you have worn those clothes to a party?" Lysander asked. "Gone barefoot?"

He had a point. "Maybe I...maybe I went home, changed my clothes, and came here."

"Drunk?" Lysander shook his head. "Have you ever done anything like that before?"

Frustrated, I stared out at the rows of gravestones. "No."

"How do you feel? Hung over? Hungry?"

"No." Which was true, now that I thought about it. I felt...fine. Perfectly fine. My head didn't hurt, my eyes didn't flinch from the bright sunlight, my stomach didn't turn from the thought of food.

"What part of your body is in that crypt, son? They haven't buried people here since the late fifties."

I glanced back at the crypt and answered without thinking. "My arm."

"Where's the rest of your body?"

I pointed west. "Over there." And east. "And there." And north. "And..." I stared at him. "I'm dead?" The shock stunned me. I couldn't seem to fit my mind around the concept.

"Yes, you're dead. Murdered, most likely. That's probably why you're here." Lysander shook his head. "You only stay behind if you have unfinished business, and I'd say yours is a slight more unfinished than any of ours."

"I'm dead?" I heard a gunshot echo in my mind. Lyle. And Brooklyn. The party. Ever so slowly, the memories began to trickle back into my waking mind. "They...they cut up my body?"

"How long will it take for anyone to notice you're gone?" Lysander asked. "Do you have a girlfriend? A wife?"

I shook my head. "I broke up with Kate a couple months ago. My rent's not due for two weeks."

"A job?"

"No, I..." I had to take a deep breath before I could continue. The panic ate into my self-control so badly that I doubted I could stand. "I got laid off a month ago."

Lysander slapped me on the shoulder. "I'm sorry, son. I really am. Let me go say goodbye to Greta, and then I'll try to answer some of your questions."

I watched him walk back to the old lady, help her up, and carefully pack up the chess set. Once she stowed it in her purse and stumped away through the maze of tombstones, Lysander walked back towards me.

"Are you dead too?" I asked. I had not moved from my spot in front of the crypt.

"I've been dead since April 17, 1955," Lysander said. "Greta visits me every day."

"She can...she can see you?"

Lysander watched her make her way to the entrance of the cemetery. "She's the reason I'm still here."

"And I'm here to find out why I was killed?" I asked.

"You don't know?" Lysander sounded more curious than saddened at the thought.

"I have no idea." I told him what had happened, hoping it would break something loose inside my mind, but the important thing I had supposedly seen refused to appear.

"Hmm." Lysander stood for a moment and mulled over what I had told him. "I'll be honest with you, son. I don't know much about this modern world, but if I were you, I'd get myself a psychic."

"A what?"

"A psychic." He seemed faintly embarrassed to be telling me this. "You know, Tarot cards and bending spoons and all."

"Why would I need a psychic?"

"They can see ghosts. There aren't all that many people who can see us, but psychics can. If you find a psychic willing to help, you might be able to find out who killed you and what they were after." He shrugged. "It's just a suggestion, son. You don't have to do a thing."

"But if I have unfinished business..."

"Some people don't much care for the thought of heaven," Lysander remarked. He indicated the young man who slept underneath the tree. "Tim's a good example; he knew exactly what he needed to do to move on, but he decided not to do it."

"So he's stuck here?" I asked, appalled.

"It's not as bad as you might think." Lysander smiled. "He spends most of the day in the library. Moving on's a matter of choice, nothing more."

I stared at the Civil War soldier for a moment, then down at my hands. "So I could stay like this for the rest of eternity?"

"You could. Being dead isn't a bad thing, really. You don't need to worry about food and clothes anymore; you don't need a place to stay..." He held out his hand and helped me stand. "There are rules, of course, but you live with rules when you're alive too."

"Rules?" It hadn't taken me much time to get used to the idea of being dead. I couldn't see that I had much choice *but* accept it; I couldn't change it.

"You can affect solid objects, but they can't affect you," Lysander said. "If you throw a rock at someone, it will hurt them, but if they throw a rock at you, it won't hurt you, even if you're solid."

"That doesn't sound too bad."

He smiled. "You can't cross running water."

"I thought that was for vampires!" My mythology was a bit rusty, but I distinctly remembered reading that somewhere.

"Them too, but they won't die if they manage to cross it," Lysander said. "The dead are tied to the land, and running water will destroy you unless you have enough self-control to fight it. I've heard of ghosts who have done it, but I don't recommend you try."

"Okay, I guess I can handle that." There was a river running through the middle of town, but I figured I could get around it somehow. I started to ask him about vampires, but then I decided I didn't really need to know. Yet. If I met any vampires, I'd ask, but I thought I should take things one day at a time.

"You can only travel five miles away from your body," Lysander said. "The dead are anchored to their bodies in ways no one really understands."

"Five miles? That's not very far."

"You shouldn't have much of a problem, since they cut you up," Lysander said. "It's a horrible thought, but they did you a favor. You should be able to instantly transport yourself to wherever your body is."

It was a *ghoulish* thought. I shivered. I felt the pull of various body parts all over the city now, as if Lysander's words had awakened the connection.

"Find yourself a psychic, son. And then decide what you want to do."

I took a deep breath even though I didn't need to. "Is there anything else I need to know?"

"Just don't let them exorcise you and you'll be fine."

I shuddered. I, like nearly every other adult in the United States, had seen *The Exorcist*. "I'll do that."

"Everything else is just a matter of concentration. You don't use up as much energy if you're not solid. Just remember that."

"Thanks."

"Come back and tell me how things are going," Lysander said. "Good luck." Before I could ask him any more questions, he vanished.

I stood for a moment and stared out at the cemetery again. My arm--however ghoulish that might seem--would be safe enough in the crypt.

I would have to make sure the rest of my body parts were just as safe.

I closed my eyes and focused on the closest one. The pull strengthened until it was almost a physical thing, and I felt a brush of wind rush past my face.

When I opened my eyes, a semi barreled straight through my body.

Lucky for the driver, I was already dead.

Chapter 3

When I was little and being a pest, my mother used to tell me to go play in traffic. I never took her seriously, of course, or I wouldn't have grown up to be murdered in my own kitchen.

Playing in traffic was not something I would recommend to anyone. Even dead, the reflexes are still there, and when I opened my eyes and saw that semi, I froze like a deer caught in headlights and didn't regain my senses until five cars and a limo had passed through me. After that first shock, getting to the sidewalk was a piece of cake. Standing in a spot where no one would walk through me was another matter entirely.

The sidewalks thronged with shoppers. It was Saturday in the big city, and everyone seemed to be out enjoying the weather. I stood for a moment, reveling in the sheer normalcy of it all, then realized I would never be part of this world again.

I walked along with the shoppers for a while, enduring the odd arm or purse through my side. It didn't hurt, but it tickled a bit. I didn't see any sign of a body part anywhere.

Noon found me sitting in a tiny park with a raggedy old man, a flock of pigeons, and a curly-haired woman playing the violin for pocket change. I sat and listened to the music for a little while, oddly at peace even though I knew I should be looking for my anchor and a psychic. The desire to find both seemed far away on a day as nice as this one.

A girl wrapped in an ugly brown coat walked across the park, scattering pigeons as she went. She ignored the old man, gave me a cursory glance, and then a classic double take. One gloved hand rose to her mouth, as if she was about to scream, then she clutched her equally ugly purse and ran out to the street. Her hair caught the sun as she hurried away, turning it into a blaze of bronze.

I didn't realize what her interest meant until I remembered that Lysander had told me we were invisible to most of the population. I ran through the pigeons, which took no notice of me, and stopped at the curb. Where had she gone?

That ugly coat gave her away. I saw her rushing down the opposite side of the street, head down and purse clutched tight against her side. She looked like a determined little bulldog, pushing past the other pedestrians without a thought for politeness.

I followed her, ignoring the 'Don't Walk' sign. By the time I reached the other side of the street, she had vanished into the crowd. I wasted the rest of the day looking for her.

I found my anchor at dusk. My killers had not been satisfied with just cutting up my body; they had cut off every identifying mark as well, it seemed. My right forefinger lay in the gutter of one of the law buildings downtown, open to the elements and already picked at by a bird or two. I didn't take it with me. Until the next rain, it would be fine where it was, and I had no true place to put a solid object.

In truth, I was a bit leery of even touching something that used to be me. The very thought of trying to find a safe place for my *body parts* was almost enough to send me screaming back to the relative safety of the cemetery.

Since the woman in the ugly brown coat had not reappeared, I decided to go psychic hunting next. I found a phone book on the corner of Main and Fourth, looked up psychics, and had a page full nearby possibilities a few minutes later. Since it was getting rather late, I decided to try Madame Zeva first. Along with Zeva, there were two Zenas, one Zabirah, a Zenobia, and a Zenith, who obviously didn't know that her name was probably a trademark infringement.

As luck would have it, the 'all-seeing, all-knowing' medium had picked this night to have a séance. I slipped through the door, warily expecting to feel some sort of unearthly power, but the air inside what looked to be a former hardware store was thick with incense and the underlying scent of bleach.

Madame Zeva had dyed her hair gypsy black. Her use of eyeliner rivaled the Ancient Egyptians. She wore what she thought a psychic should wear...a flounced red skirt and a white peasant blouse that showed enough cleavage to irritate the women, and interest the men, in the audience. The large gold loops in her ears were tarnished brass, and the rings on her fingers were about as authentic as the crystal ball on the table in front of her.

I had my doubts she could help me at all. I tried to get her attention by waving my hand in front of her face, but she ignored me in favor of adopting a thick accent that impressed her followers and disgusted me.

"Join handz around ze table," she intoned, fluttering her fake eyelashes at the youngest member of the party.

His girlfriend frowned and took his hand possessively. I leaned back against the wall to watch. One of the older women giggled nervously when the lights dimmed by themselves; I, on the other hand, was not impressed.

"Ve have come here to contact the dead, no?" Madame Zeva asked. "I vill see eef ze currents are sympathetic tonight." I noticed a cigar box, with a hole cut into the top, sitting behind the crystal ball. I didn't realize what it was until Madame Zeva reached across the table to shake the box. "Oh, spirits of ze undervorld, are zese offerings enough for zee?"

From out of a speaker, disguised as a chandelier, a voice thundered a negative. It sounded vaguely European, and I wondered how much she had paid to get the recording. With a nudge from their wives, the older men in the circle took out their wallets and added to the pot. The younger boy frowned at his girlfriend's whispered insistence, then put a five through the slot. Even though Madame Zeva's eyes were closed, I thought I saw a sliver of white showing. She was milking them for all they had.

This time, the offering was acceptable. Madame Zeva moaned and fluttered her eyes, evidently in the throes of ghostly possession. The thought of actually possessing her never really crossed my mind; Lysander hadn't gone into that and I had no desire to try.

I almost left, but the temptation was just too great. As soon as she had stopped moaning, and had lowered her head against her chest, feigning exhaustion, I lifted the offering box, shook it, then dumped it out onto the table. Coins and scattered bills flew everywhere.

The participants watched in stunned awe. Madame Zeva raised her head when she heard the jingle of falling change. She goggled at the upturned box, recovered quickly, and smiled weakly at her customers.

"Ze spirits, zey are playful tonight." She cast a quick glance to each corner of the room, as if expecting some prankster to be hiding in the shadows. Her gaze passed right over me.

I guess I shouldn't have been so surprised. There were shysters in every profession, after all. Finding a real psychic might be more difficult than I had at first expected. An image of the woman in the ugly brown coat rose up in my mind. I'd have to try to find her again, but in a city this size, it would not be easy.

I stayed for the rest of the séance, but I was too depressed to do anything but watch. Playing with the lights or making the crystal ball float would have been amusing, in a macabre sense, but even Madame Zeva had to make a living, and I had no right to frighten her or anyone else by playing poltergeist. I didn't bother to track down the rest of the psychics; I had a feeling they'd turn out to be just as fake.

Chapter 4

After the disaster with Madame Zeva, I decided to visit the scene of the crime next. I had to walk the whole way, since none of my body parts seemed to be within two miles of my former home, but I enjoyed the walk. I didn't have to be wary of the dark anymore; no one in their right mind would try to mug a dead man.

Getting through the door wasn't a problem. Forcing myself to look at the spot where I had died...I avoided the kitchen, walked into the living room, and gaped at the mess.

Someone had completely trashed my apartment. Books, Records, CDs, and tapes lay scattered and broken across the floor. My signed Journey album had been torn to pieces. All of my videotapes had been pulled out and cut.

In the bedroom, things were worse. Someone had sliced through the mattress and sheets, scattering stuffing all around the room. My clothes lay in a rumpled heap on the floor; the bathroom mirror had been smashed.

I sat down on the edge of the ruined bed and stared at the destruction. My whole life had been ruined because I had seen something I wasn't supposed to see. Murdering me was one thing; I thought I could accept that, now that I was a ghost, but destroying all my stuff? *That* sucked.

A photo of my parents lay on the bedroom floor, half covered by broken glass. I knelt in front of it and tried to pick it up. My fingers went right through it. With a little concentration, though, I managed to think my fingers solid enough to brush the glass off the photograph and pick it up. What would they think of me now? Who would tell them I was dead?

Someone opened my front door. The sound didn't register for a long moment, and when I finally realized I was no longer alone, I let the photo fall and struggled to my feet.

"We have to get this cleaned up," I heard a woman say. "If the landlord gets suspicious..."

"Do you think they found it yet?" This person sounded young enough to be carded if he tried to buy anything harder than Mountain Dew. I slipped around the corner and silently made my way down the hall.

"I doubt it. Sheridan would have announced his triumph and the city would be in ruins. He's not that subtle."

Who was Sheridan? I had never seen the woman standing in the kitchen, but she looked oddly familiar anyway, as if I had seen her breathtaking beauty on the cover of a magazine at the grocery store. She stood a half a head taller than me, and wore a silky red shirt that left absolutely nothing to the imagination. Her jeans hugged her hips like a second skin, and her hair caught the light as if it were on fire. She wore no makeup, save for lipstick that matched her shirt exactly, and fiery red nail polish on her long nails.

Her companion, on the other hand, was a slight, bespectacled young boy who couldn't have been more than sixteen. He wore his black hair fashionably long, and his clothing was equally fashionable--baggy jeans and a t-shirt two sizes too large. He carried a laptop case and a tote bag. The woman's hands were empty.

I stayed out of sight, just in case they could see me. Maybe, just maybe, they were involved in this mess and would leave me some clues to work with.

"I wish we could have done this earlier," the woman said. "What if someone had dropped by?"

"From what I could tell, Will Spark was a bit of a loner," the boy said dispassionately. "He liked to drink, liked to party, and didn't have much of a life outside of that." He checked a small notebook. "He broke up with his girlfriend two months ago, but she has not tried to contact him since then."

"Then why is the answering machine light flashing?" the woman asked. She pressed the button, but it was only a salesman trying to sell me new windows. "What about family? Did he have any? Are they going to be a problem?"

"Perhaps." The boy shrugged. "It's hard to tell."

It was no secret that I liked to drink, especially if I didn't have to pay for it, but this boy's quiet summation of my life struck me as unfair. I hadn't *always* been a good-for-nothing out of work loser. Once upon a time, I'd had dreams of being a drummer in a rock band, but that had never come to pass.

And now it never would. I followed them through the apartment, increasingly depressed. Did it matter if I "moved on"? Should I even try to figure out why I was killed and what I had seen?

The boy stopped in every room and sketched a small picture of how the room had looked before my killers had trashed the place. I watched with cautious interest, bolder now that neither of them had noticed me, and stood over his shoulder as he set his computer up on the kitchen table and plugged it in. The tote bag held a small scanner, and he used it to scan his drawings into a program I did not recognize. He tapped a few keys, moved the mouse around a bit, and slowly an image of my apartment appeared on the screen. I saw my bed, my dresser, my couch; all my furniture picked up and placed back into their proper places.

The woman left for a little while, then returned with a list of every single book, videotape, CD, and record I owned. The boy scanned that list in as well, and entered it into his program.

"You might want to sit down for this part, Maeve. I'm not sure how long it will take."

I watched, fascinated, as he called up a string of shifting numbers on the screen. He typed in a bevy of commands, pressed enter twice, then sat back and smiled at the woman.

Maeve, I remembered. An unusual name. I noticed he seemed quite pale, suddenly, as if the computer program ran from his strength instead of electricity. He removed his glasses, closed his eyes, and rubbed the bridge of his nose.

"Are you okay?" Maeve asked.

The boy nodded. "I'll be fine once this is over. It's...tiring for me." Was it my imagination, or did his gaze flicker towards me for a moment? I faded back into the other room, but still watched the computer screen.

"If Sheridan finds the phoenix, none of us will have anything to worry about," Maeve said grimly. "We'll all be dead."

I didn't like the sound of Sheridan at all. I watched the computer screen shift and pulse. Was this why I had been killed? For a phoenix? Vague memories of long-ago required reading drifted through my mind. A phoenix. Some sort of mythical bird...

"Not if we get it first," the boy replied, smiling at her. The smile faded before it reached his eyes.

Maeve didn't look very pleased at the thought, but she did not disagree with him.

The computer beeped. The boy exhaled and replaced his glasses. He unplugged it from the wall, carefully stowed everything away in his bag, and stood. "Are you ready?"

"Should we make sure everything worked?" Maeve asked. "Not that I don't trust you, Justin, but..."

"It worked." Justin motioned to the part of the kitchen I couldn't allow myself to see. "The blood is gone."

The blood *was* gone. In fact, the entire proof of my murder had been completely erased. The couch stood back against the wall, my albums stood unbroken in their cases. Everything had been put back exactly as it had been before my death.

Well, not quite exactly. As I stood in the doorway of the kitchen and stared at my clean apartment, I realized that Justin had not only put everything back, he had cleaned the dirty dishes, steam cleaned the carpet, and vanquished the spider webs from the corners of each and every room.

My apartment looked brand new. I was still staring when Maeve and Justin let themselves out, and by the time I recovered enough to follow them, they were gone.

I had managed to collect a few precious scraps of information from their conversation, but I had no idea what any of it meant. And I had even less of an idea what I could do with the information I had gathered.

Chapter 5

Whatever leads Maeve and Justin had given me would not work unless I had more information. I left my apartment and decided to retrace my steps back to Larry's house, in the hopes that I would find out what I had supposedly seen. If I knew that, I had a feeling most of my missing pieces would fall into place.

The streets were deserted at this time of night, and I had the entire block to myself. Two cars passed, but otherwise the neighborhood was silent and still, caught in the spell of some unimaginable enchantment. I took my time, peering into alleys and into darkened windows, trying to jog my memory loose.

Two blocks away from Larry's house, I passed a dark alley that smelled as if it had been the nesting place of a dozen trolls. I stepped into it gingerly, expecting the gunk on the ground to squish under my feet, but my passage left no mark at all on the debris. Rusting garbage cans overflowing with moldy food and bags of newspapers choked one side of the alley and the hulk of what looked to be a Toyota clogged the other side. Two sets of footprints, one going in and one going out marked the passageway through the two piles. Were those my footprints? Unlike now, I hadn't been able to see in the dark last night. What would have possessed me to walk into a stinking alley? What had I seen?

When I stepped around the car and the garbage, a flash of blue caught my eye. It wasn't a *usual* color in an alley, especially not in the dark. I knelt in the muck and concentrated on solidity. Moving the piled newspapers took an ungodly amount of strength, and when I finally threw away the last one, I felt only disappointment.

The blue flash had been from a blue jay feather. I wasn't quite sure how I had noticed the blue when it had been completely covered by the newspapers, but I had seen *something*, and this feather was the only blue thing I had found.

What was a blue jay doing in the city? I had never seen one in all my years of living there; the birds I noticed were the pigeons, the starlings, and the odd peregrine falcon. Not blue jays. Blue jays belonged in the country, with my childhood memories of my grandparents' farm.

I reached down, picked up the feather, and twirled it between my fingers. Just a feather. I had been so sure I'd find some clue, and I had found a feather.

And not very pretty one at that. There was something on it that sparkled in the moonlight, clinging to each individual strand of blue, black and white. I touched the stuff with the tip of my finger and the feather burst into flame.

I forgot to concentrate on solidity. The feather fell through my hand, leaving a slight stinging sensation in its wake, and drifted to the ground. As soon as it hit the muck, it stopped burning and lay there innocently, looking for all the world like an innocent feather.

I stared down at it. Maeve had said something about a phoenix, and the dregs of my memory supplied more information that I realized I knew about them. I would have to find a book and look it up to be sure, but weren't phoenixes the birds that burst into flames?

I bent down and picked up the feather again. It didn't burst into flames this time, but burned with a steady and non-consuming fire as soon as I touched it.

Perhaps I had found a clue after all. Staying solid was an effort, but I managed to get the feather back to my apartment without dropping it again. I ran into a bit of a problem when I realized the door was shut and locked, but the feather passed through the door without a hitch.

I stuck it inside of a clean pickle jar, then stowed the jar at the very back of my sock drawer for want of a better hiding place. I spent an hour or two trying to write down what I knew, but retrieving the feather had used up most of my strength. I managed to fall asleep before dawn.

My dreams were of Maeve and her fiery hair.

Chapter 6

I spent the next morning at the library. Tim was already there; he gave me a half-wave when I walked through the door, but there were no living patrons this early in the morning. The librarians didn't notice either of us, even though the books Tim carried from the shelves had to be floating on air.

"You're Will," he said as soon as I approached.

"Yeah."

"Lysander wanted me to tell you to be careful. Evidently there were some people nosing around the cemetery last night."

"Did he say what they looked like?" I asked.

Tim shrugged. "A kid and a red-haired woman. He said they knew right where your arm is, but they didn't disturb it."

Maeve and Justin. Who were they? Why had they erased all evidence of my murder? Were they working in tandem with Lyle and Brooklyn, or were they working for someone else? Sheridan perhaps? Maeve hadn't sounded very fond of Sheridan, whoever he was.

"I know their names, but I don't know who they are," I said. "They were in my apartment last night."

"Strange to revisit the scene of a crime," Tim commented.

"I've never seen them before," I said. "I'm not sure where they fit in." And I had a schedule to keep if I planned on finding more clues today. "Do you know if the library has any books on phoenixes?" I asked.

"Try the mythology section," Tim suggested. "Greek myths, I think. Or ask a librarian; they're usually pretty receptive."

I found what I was looking for an hour later. The Phoenix--evidently there was only one living at any time--was the rarest mythical bird in the world. There were conflicting stories about how it reproduced, but most of the stories agreed on one thing: phoenixes burned to death and left an egg behind. They were said to resemble both sparrows and birds-of-paradise. I found no mention of blue jays.

Did I have a phoenix feather in a pickle jar in my sock drawer, or had I been hallucinating? The feather had still been burning this morning when I left, but the flame did not give off any heat that I could detect. The books did not say one word about that, of course.

I committed as much information as I could to memory, re-shelved the books, then turned to go. Out of the corner of my eye, I saw someone duck out of sight as I turned...and that someone was much too short to be Tim.

I had the advantage over anyone living attempting to escape my notice. I slid through three bookcases, turned a corner, and came face to face with Justin.

He yelped and jumped back against the wall when I appeared in front of him, but he had nowhere to go unless he wanted to go through me. I saw the possibility fly through his mind, and then he wilted, too frightened to actually try it.

"You can see me." It wasn't a question, but I wanted an answer. Today, he looked even younger than he had last night, and there were dark rings under his eyes.

He sighed and slumped back against the wall. "Yeah. I can see you. You're Will Spark, aren't you?"

"Could you see me last night?" I asked.

Justin nodded. "I didn't want Maeve to know. You being a ghost really screws up her plans, you know?"

I didn't know, but I could pretend with the best of them. "Why don't you tell me about her plans?" I asked. "Knowing a bit more about why I was murdered and chopped into little bits would help too."

Justin flushed. "Would you believe me if I told you that you were in the wrong place at the right time?" he asked. "It's kind of hard to explain."

"I have the rest of eternity, as far as I know." I folded my arms and tried to look angry. It was hard; Justin was a cute kid.

He flushed again. "I don't know if I should be telling you this..."

"If I'm involved, I need to know."

He chewed on his lower lip for a moment, then sighed. "Do you want to go to lunch? Maeve won't be back for me until dark and Rose is...well..." He shrugged. "Rose thinks I'm in school."

"And why aren't you in school?" I asked.

"I saw you last night in your apartment, and the psychic emanations from the cemetery made me..."

I held up my hands. "Whoa. Wait a second. Psychic what? You're talking to a beginner here, kid, so try to speak English."

"Emanations. I felt your presence in the cemetery last night."

"I wasn't in the cemetery last night." Maybe some people could understand all this psychic/supernatural stuff right off the bat, but I was having a hard time swallowing it all. Being dead was bad enough, but magical computer programs? Phoenixes? Where would it end?

Justin sighed. "I know. But you were there at one time, weren't you?"

"When I woke up like *this*," I said. "When I realized my *arm* was in that crypt..."

Justin flushed again. I wondered if he had anything to do with the disposal of my body. Surely Brooklyn and Lyle had not forced him to help.

"I don't blame you for being confused," he said. "Do you want to talk over lunch?"

"I don't eat," I said, unable to resist another barb. "But if you promise to answer some questions...yeah. I'll go to lunch with you."

We ended up at a fast food restaurant downtown, not far away from my finger. I would have bought the kid lunch if I had any money, but Justin was forced to order his own. I was only half-surprised that he ordered breakfast instead of lunch.

"How much did you overhear last night?" Justin asked as soon as he poured syrup on his hotcakes.

"A bunch of stuff I don't understand," I said. "Something about a phoenix, and someone named Sheridan who seems to want it." I debated whether to tell him about my feather or not, and decided to keep quiet for the time being. Even though Justin was a kid, I didn't know if I could trust him. Anyone mixed up in this mess was suspect in my mind.

Justin glanced around the empty restaurant when I spoke Sheridan's name, as if he expected the man to step out from behind the counter and pounce on both of us. "Sheridan. Yeah. He's actually my..." He started and stared in horror at something behind my back.

I turned.

The woman in the ugly brown coat stood behind me, her lips pressed together in a thin, hard line. She wore a knitted purple hat that clashed horribly with her hair. Despite the clothes, she was quite lovely, and I finally realized where I had seen Maeve's face before.

"Hi, Aunt Rose," Justin said weakly.

The woman looked me up and down, her eyes narrowed. She stood for a moment, staring at both of us, then held one hand out in an obvious order. Justin abandoned his breakfast and slipped past me to grab her hand.

"*You* will leave my nephew alone." Her order only riled my temper. When she turned away from me, I hurried after her.

"Look, lady, I didn't do a thing to your nephew. He followed *me*. I just want to know what's going on."

"What's going on is no concern of yours," Rose said sharply. "Begone before I banish you, spirit."

"She can do it; I've seen her," Justin confirmed.

I stepped back, but I couldn't just leave well enough alone. "Look. Just let me talk to him. I swear to you I won't harm a hair on his head. I just want to know why he was in my apartment last night."

I caught Justin's frantic look a second too late. Rose slowed, then stopped. She stared down at her nephew, then back at me. Out of the corner of my eye, I saw the two restaurant workers staring from behind the counter at the crazy woman and her equally crazy nephew.

"Justin, were you in this man's apartment last night?" If Rose had been a teacher, she could have snapped her students into shape with just one sentence in that tone of voice. I felt myself bristle in protest.

Justin lowered his gaze to the floor. "Yes, Aunt Rose."

"With Maeve?" I'd thought her voice cold before, but when she uttered Maeve's name, she froze Hell.

Justin sighed. "Yes, Aunt Rose."

"What exactly did you do?" She wasn't yelling, exactly, but her tone of voice left no room for argument or lies. I felt sorry for Justin. If he had to put up with this all the time...

"Maeve said if we fixed his apartment, the landlord wouldn't call the police. If no one saw the blood."

I risked a glance at our audience to see what they thought of this new development. The manager had his hand on the phone, ready to call the police.

"The blood."

"I was murdered two nights ago," I offered. "Someone cut up my body and stashed it all over the city."

Rose glared at me. "I didn't ask *you*. Be quiet."

Obviously, Rose had something against ghosts. I folded my arms and leaned back against a booth, content to wait.

Rose glared at me again, then returned her gaze to her hapless nephew. "And how, exactly, did you clean up the mess?"

Justin bit his lip and looked away.

Rose grabbed his arm. "Justin! You didn't."

"Maeve said she'd stop if I got too tired, Aunt Rose."

"Damn her." Rose's face went from pale to scarlet in an instant. "Damn her to hell."

"Aunt Rose..."

And now, it was my turn to feel her fury. Rose turned on me, one hand upraised. Justin tried to tug on her arm to stop her, but she shook him away and twisted the lid off a small bottle of what looked like holy water.

Holy water? Visions of exorcism danced through my mind. I did the only thing I could. I reached out to an anchor, closed my eyes, and pulled myself to safety with the beginnings of a phrase of Latin echoing in my ears.

Chapter 7

"You look like you've seen a ghost." Lysander laughed at his own joke and slapped me on the back. I opened my eyes cautiously, expecting to see Rose standing in front of me with that bottle of holy water, but I saw the peaceful cemetery again. No Rose. No Justin. And damn it all, no new clues.

"I was just about to get exorcised, I think," I said, and slid off the crypt. "I've met some interesting people since I died."

"Did Tim find you?" Lysander asked. "I sent him along with a message."

"Yeah. About Maeve and Justin."

"You know them?"

I shrugged. "Not really, but they seem to be involved with my murder. They...cleaned my apartment last night. With some sort of weird computer program. Or magic. I couldn't quite decide."

Lysander raised one eyebrow. "A computer program?"

"Computer...magic...I have no idea. The kid pressed a button and my apartment looked better than new."

"Did they see you?"

"Justin did, but I didn't know it at the time. He was about to tell me everything he knew when his Aunt Rose showed up, and I..."

"Rose?" The woman in black with the cigarette showed an interest in me for the first time. "Not Rose Winter?"

"I don't know," I said. "I didn't catch her last name." *And she wasn't about to give it to me.*

"Describe her to me."

I even included the ugly brown coat in my description. The woman pursed her lips.

"Hmm. It sounds like Rose. Did I hear you say Maeve?"

"Her sister?" I guessed.

The woman nodded. "The next time you see Rose, tell her Marla's still waiting to talk to her. Will you do that for me?"

I glanced at Lysander. "I thought you said no one has been buried here since the late fifties."

"Oh, they haven't, honey." Marla sucked on her cigarette and blew out a stream of smoke. "I'm not buried in the cemetery."

"Where are you buried?"

"That's not a polite thing to ask a lady," Lysander whispered, but I ignored him.

Marla motioned with her cigarette. "See that tree across the street?" The tree in question was an old, twisted oak that dominated the landscape. Half of it had been burned by lightning, and the living half only caused the dead half to look even worse. "If you walk three paces behind that tree, you'll find a brick. I'm buried under that brick." She tapped ghostly ash onto the tombstone beside her. "I only came here to get away from that wretched tree."

"Oh, I see." Evidently, there were more hidden bodies in the city than I had expected. "What does Rose have to do with that?"

Marla gave me a nicotine stained smile. "Her father murdered me twenty-three years ago, the year Rose was born."

"Her father murdered you?" I glanced at Lysander, who closed his eyes and shook his head. "His name wouldn't happen to be Sheridan, would it?"

Marla laughed. "What's Sheridan up to these days?"

For some reason, I didn't want to tell Marla about the phoenix, if there even *was* a phoenix. "I'm not sure. His name came up last night."

"Sheridan O'Rourke is Maeve's father," Marla said quietly. "Him and that no-good wife of his are never up to any good, if you ask me." She took a furious drag on her cigarette and sighed.

"So Maeve and Rose are only half-sisters?" I asked, trying to keep things straight.

"I'm not sure. Officially, they're half-sisters, but I always thought they looked too much alike. After Howard got rid of me to marry sweet, little Emily Marchand, I didn't keep track of them until Howard died less than a year later."

"Emily married Sheridan O'Rourke?"

"Emily inherited my husband's money, sold off his house in Miami and gave birth to Maeve six months later."

"But Maeve's not Howard's daughter?" I honestly didn't see what this had to do with my problem at all, but I didn't want to walk away from a possible clue.

Marla laughed. Her laugh was as hoarse as her voice, no doubt due to the cigarettes. The one in the holder never seemed to burn down, and I wondered if she had ever tried to quit. I was more of a drinker than a smoker, but I hadn't had the urge for a beer ever since I woke up dead. I wondered how long that would last.

"You've never seen Sheridan O'Rourke, have you? Both girls inherited the O'Rourke red hair, although Rose's is a bit darker than Maeve's, and

Sheridan's is white now, of course. The Marchand family is very strenuously blond. My husband didn't have anything but brown in his family." She leered. "I thought it was a bit obvious."

I thought a family history was a bit much to declare adultery, but I held my tongue. I didn't want to go back to the city just yet. I wanted to give Rose a chance to cool off first, and then try to find Justin again.

"If they come back here, do you want me to tell you?" Lysander asked. "I'm here all the time."

"I'd appreciate it."

"No problem." Lysander glanced towards the cemetery gates and I realized Greta had not been with him when I arrived.

"Where's Greta?"

"I don't know," Lysander confessed. "She's usually here right at noon, but today..." He sighed. "I think I'd know it if she died, wouldn't you think?"

"Would you like me to go look for her?" Looking for a little old lady would keep my mind off of Maeve, Rose, and Justin for a little while. I thought I could use a bit of a distraction.

Lysander's smile was full of pure relief. "Would you? I'd go myself, but I'm not supposed to leave."

"Whose rules?" I asked.

"Each and every cemetery in this city has a resident ghost who takes care of new recruits and keeps the cemetery nice and neat. Tim was that person until I got here; no one else wanted to do it, and he hadn't left the cemetery in almost eighty years." He shrugged. "It doesn't usually bother me, but today..."

"I'll find her," I promised. "Will she be able to see me?"

"Without a doubt."

He gave me her address, thanked me again, and watched me until I had walked out of sight.

Chapter 8

The walk to Greta's house let me think about how I had handled my encounter with Justin and Rose. I could have been nicer to both of them. I'd chased the kid, snapped at his aunt, and basically made an ass out of myself without even trying. Rose hadn't behaved very well either, but I couldn't blame it all on her. I resolved to apologize the next time I saw her, but I didn't think it would help her mood any. It was quite obvious that she didn't like ghosts.

It took me almost an hour to find the address Lysander had given me, and at first I thought he had given me the wrong address. 1620 Currier Lane was not the quaint little cottage I expected Greta to be living in. It seemed to be a tattoo parlor and a bar in one. The sign on the door said 'We Ink While You Drink'. I tried not to groan when I walked through the door.

I stood for a moment to orient myself, then realized I had a slight problem with my plan. I couldn't ask anyone about Greta; they couldn't see me. I had not thought of that.

I prowled around anyway, watched a cute blond getting a fairy tattooed on her lower back, then drifted up a rickety pair of stairs. Greta's apartment was the first one on my left.

And Lysander had been right to worry. The shrunken form laying under the spotless blankets bore no resemblance to the tiny old lady I had seen in the cemetery. This old lady's breath rattled in her lungs and her eyes were sunken deep into her wrinkled face. The room stank of old lady and death. I hurried downstairs and tried to get the attention of one of the bartenders, but they ignored my frantic shouts in favor of a sitcom rerun on television. When I went solid enough to turn off the TV, they merely turned it back on and accused each other of treachery. When I pushed a full bottle of Jack Daniel's off the counter, the older bartender called the younger one a clumsy ass and forced him to clean up the mess. I guess I could have tried harder to get their attention, but neither man cared about the old lady upstairs.

I saw a pay phone hanging on the wall and wondered if Rose's number would be listed. She was the only living person, save for Justin, who could see me, and while I didn't trust her, I doubted she was heartless enough to let an old lady die alone.

I flipped through the W's until I found Winter, then ran my finger down the rows until I found Rose. I had no change, so I had to call her collect.

"What do *you* want?" She didn't sound like she had calmed down at all. I gripped the phone, struggling to stay solid, and prayed I could get her to call 911.

"Rose, Ms. Winter, I wouldn't have called if it wasn't an emergency. I know you don't like me very much..."

She snorted. "At all is more like it."

"Okay, I'll give you that. You don't like me at all. But I met a nice old guy at a cemetery not too far away when I woke up like this. He plays chess with his wife every day. Her name is Greta."

"Lysander Perkins?" Rose asked. Her voice warmed enough for the glaciers to begin to melt. "I've heard of Lysander and Greta. They're...well, kind of celebrities."

"Greta didn't come to the cemetery today," I said. "Lysander can't leave; he's the guardian or something, so I said I'd find Greta and make sure she was okay."

"Has she died?" Rose actually sounded sorry.

"Not yet. I need you to call 911, Rose, and tell them to come to this address." I recited the address to her and hoped she wrote it down. "I can't hold onto the phone for much longer. I haven't gotten the hang of this solid thing yet."

"You want *me* to call 911. That's all you want." Rose didn't sound like she believed me.

"Please. I'd do it myself, but they wouldn't be able to hear me."

"That's it? That's all you want?"

"Yes." Getting answers could wait. Greta would be dead if I delayed any longer, and I did not want to have to inform Lysander of her death.

Rose's voice softened. "I'll call them. Are you going to stay with her?"

"Yeah, I'd better go to the hospital with her, too. I can get back to Lysander as soon as I know if she's going to make it."

Rose had hung up before I finished speaking. I stared at the phone for a moment, then hung it back up and made my way back upstairs.

Greta had not changed. Twenty minutes later, when the EMTs arrived, loaded her onto a stretcher and carted her away, I snuck on board the ambulance and sat beside her, not even realizing we would cross a bridge until I felt the mad disorientation of the water attack my senses and throw me away.

Unable to stand the displacement, I reached for an anchor, found one, and felt the horrible sickness recede.

When I opened my eyes, I found I stood in a child's bedroom. Posters of various movie monsters decorated the walls; models of the same monsters lined the heavily laden bookshelves. A familiar looking laptop sat on a small desk, and behind that laptop sat a very familiar boy.

Justin glanced up as soon as I appeared. "Ah." He pressed a button on his computer and I felt something strong and invisible fix me into place, as if he had somehow created a net to trap ghosts. He typed something into the computer and the invisible bands tightened until they actually became painful. I tried to struggle, but struggling only made it worse.

"I'm sorry to do this to you, Mr. Spark, but Maeve will want to talk to you when she wakes up." He tapped a key and the bands loosened only a fraction, but enough for me to speak.

"Justin, I have to get to the hospital! You have to let me go." I'd never been very good at begging, but I was begging now.

Justin shut the computer case with an air of finality. "I'm not going to let you go. Don't bother to ask. There's only four hours left until dawn; you can wait that long." His face had turned a shade of sickly gray and sweat broke out across his forehead. He breathed heavily through his nose and stared at the top of the computer for a moment, as if steeling himself to stand.

"What's wrong with you?" I asked. "Why does...the magic affect you this way?"

Justin sighed. "I'm cursed. That's all you need to know."

I stared at him. His eyes weren't focusing right, but he didn't seem to notice...yet. I pushed at my invisible bonds. Justin's face turned white.

Whatever he did; whatever spell he cast, directly affected his health. I saw that now as I hadn't quite seen it before. Each spell Justin cast weakened him further and further. They would continue weakening him until...until what? Until he died? Until he found a way to break the curse?

"Justin, I'm not going to stop fighting this. You'll be unconscious before I'm finished."

Justin sat in stone-faced silence, glowering at the computer.

"What will your Aunt Rose say if she knew you had done this? Can't I make you a bargain?"

Justin let out his breath in a rush. "What kind of bargain?"

"I need to find a way to the hospital that doesn't involve crossing water," I said. "Once I make sure Greta's okay, I'll come back here and talk to you and Maeve. I *swear* to you, Justin. I'll come back."

"If you don't come back, I'll have Aunt Rose banish you," Justin growled. With shaking hands he opened the computer again and typed in a string of words and numbers. I felt the bonds loosen, almost enough for me to escape.

Justin grew steadily weaker as he typed. Unmaking the spell seemed to drain him faster than creating it, and he was visibly drooping when the bonds finally fell away.

I stepped forward, intending to thank him, but before I could open my mouth, he slid from his chair and landed in a heap on the floor.

I hesitated. I desperately needed to get to the hospital, but I couldn't leave Justin lying there either. For all I knew, his curse had side effects I didn't want to imagine, and I didn't want to be responsible for his death. I glanced around for something--anything--I could use to summon Rose and not get into trouble.

Rose made that decision for me. She walked into Justin's room without knocking, a basket of laundry blocking her view of both Justin and me.

"Justin? I brought your..." When she stepped on his outstretched hand, she realized something was wrong. And when she saw me, she deduced, wrongly, that I had been at fault.

This time, when I fled her Latin phrases, I took care to use the anchor nearest to the hospital. By the time I found Greta and determined that she wasn't going to die just yet, it was almost dusk.

First, the cemetery, then I'd see about keeping my promise to Justin. If I appeared in his room again and Rose was there with her holy water, I didn't even want to attempt it. But if Justin had awakened and told her what we had agreed on, I had a good chance at staying earthbound for another evening.

Either way, if I didn't hurry, I wouldn't make it anywhere. I closed my eyes, located my arm, and pulled myself back to where Lysander waited.

Chapter 9

An hour later, I pulled myself back to Justin's room, weary in both body and soul. At that moment, I honestly did not care if Rose met me with holy water and the Pope himself.

The hospital was twenty miles away from the cemetery. Lysander's face had frozen at the news, and I had no way to help him. I alone had an anchor close enough to the hospital to see Greta, and short of exhuming Lysander's body and taking a bone with me, I did not know what else to do.

Tim had offered to resume his post as guardian if I found a way to allow Lysander to leave. I had left for my meeting with Maeve and Justin shortly after that. I had no idea how I would be able to persuade them to dig up a forty-seven-year old body so an old man could be with his wife until the end.

Neither Rose nor Justin waited for me when I opened my eyes. The laptop was gone from the little desk, and Justin's bed had not been slept in. I hesitated before gliding through the door, not sure what I would find on the other side, but the entire house was silent and still. No one seemed to be home.

Had I come too late? I glanced out the window and saw the faintest smear of pink against the night sky; the remnants of a spectacular sunset I'd been too busy to enjoy. I sighed and drifted through the kitchen wall. At least I could leave them a note, or something, to reassure Justin I had not broken my promise.

A muffled sound outside of the patio doors caught my attention, and I saw a bird fluttering helplessly against the glass, fighting to get in. I stared at it for a moment, puzzled, and then I realized why it looked so strange.

It was a blue jay, but not a blue jay. The colors smeared and spread across its back as I watched, changing from blue to green to purple. The bird grew before my eyes, becoming as large as a parrot, then shrinking to the size of a tiny hummingbird. When it realized it was being watched, it stopped fluttering, stared up at me, unafraid, and chirped.

I almost forgot to go solid when I fumbled for the latch on the door. The phoenix--if that is what it was--hopped through the door and fluttered its wings. I concentrated, held out my arm, and offered it to the bird. It flew up to inspect my offering, moved around a bit until it was comfortable, and settled in for a nice long stay.

I had no idea if I could stay solid for that long, so I searched around for a place for it to perch. Rose had a rounded banana holder on the counter, sans bananas, and I carried the phoenix over to it and tried to be patient as it maneuvered its way down my arm. It had just gripped the banana stand with one claw when I heard a footstep behind me.

I spun around.

"I thought you'd be along eventually," Maeve said, drop-dead gorgeous in a tiny teddy that showed more leg than a naked turkey. She wore a filmy black scrap of material over it all, but that only made matters worse. Her hair flowed over her shoulders. I wanted to run my fingers through that hair so badly that I stepped towards her and had actually raised my hand before the phoenix's chirp brought me out of my daze. I stepped back, confused.

Maeve laughed. "It's a shame you're dead, Will Spark. It would have been fun getting to know you. I see you've found the phoenix."

"It found me," I admitted. "I thought you couldn't see ghosts."

"Do you know where Rose and Justin are?" She sashayed over to a cluttered bulletin board and searched amid the expired coupons and ancient reminders for the note that wasn't there. "They usually leave me a note." She smiled back at me. "I can see ghosts when I want to, but I never expected to see *you* again. Were you eavesdropping on us last night? I thought I felt something."

I explained what had happened to Justin earlier, but she didn't seem to be very worried.

"Justin can take care of himself. Rose babies him too much." She shook her head and her hair swept across her back. My fingers itched. The phoenix glowered at me.

"I actually came here for your help," I admitted. "I need you to exhume a grave."

"A grave?" She did not turn around. "Justin and I made sure you were well-scattered, Will. I doubt you'll ever be able to find all the pieces." She spun around as soon as she said that, her hand over her mouth. "Oh, hell. I didn't mean to say that."

"*You* chopped up my body?" I couldn't imagine Maeve cutting up anything more difficult than a boneless chicken breast.

"I had to do something," she replied. "I couldn't just leave you there and let the police investigate. Do you realize what that bird means? We've won."

"As far as I'm concerned, you haven't won a thing," I snapped. "It came to me, not you."

"That's right, of course it did," Maeve seemed to have forgotten my presence. "It came to you because you were the first person to see it when it arrived. And even though you're dead, you're still present, so you're still its guardian."

"It's what?" I asked. She had lost me back at the 'first person to see it' sentence. I had no idea what she was talking about. "Look. I read all the books in the library about phoenixes. Not one of those books said anything about guardians."

"Oh, it's true enough," Maeve said. "I've read the same book Sheridan has, and he's the one who predicted the phoenix's arrival." She opened the fridge, took out a corked bottle of what looked like runny ketchup, and poured herself a glass. She popped the glass into the microwave, set it on high, and stared at the phoenix until it was finished. "I'm not trying to be rude, but you really wouldn't want any of this. Believe me."

"I'm dead. I haven't wanted a drink in three days." Had it really only been three days? I counted backwards in my mind. It *had* only been three days. It seemed like I had been dead for three *years*.

Maeve smiled and took a long drink. "I imagine not." She indicated the phoenix. "So what are you going to do with it? How are you going to feed it? Where is it going to stay?"

"I..." I glanced at the phoenix, but it gave me no clues. I wanted to tell her I had it all figured out, but I hadn't even thought that far ahead. Maeve was right. Where *would* I keep a mythical bird? How would I feed it? How could *I* be its guardian?

"Whose grave did you want me to exhume?" Maeve asked. "If I dig up the grave, will you agree to listen to a proposal?"

I glanced at the phoenix again, but it did not move. The colors had settled down to a moderate mix of reds, blues and greens, but it was unlike any parrot I had ever seen. It had a bright blue beak, a red-feathered head with two streaks of royal blue on either side of its eyes. One wing had mostly green feathers, the other mostly blue. Its tail feathers were long, curled, and a vivid green. It was the strangest looking bird I'd ever seen.

"You'll exhume the grave and I only have to listen to a proposal?" I asked. "And what if I don't accept the proposal?"

"Then Sheridan will find out you're still around. When he finds out you have the phoenix, he'll call in every exorcist in the city to make sure you can't prosper from your good fortune."

I hesitated.

Maeve's smile was grim. "Believe me, Will Spark. Sheridan O'Rourke will stop at nothing to get what he wants. If he has to exorcise every cemetery in the city to get you to comply with his wishes, he will. Have no doubt about that."

"And if I agree to your proposal?"

"You haven't heard it yet," Maeve said. "I suggest we discuss this in detail after I exhume this grave for you. Who's in it?"

I explained Lysander's plight. Maeve stared at me for a moment, and then shook her head.

"If I had known you were this conscientious, I never would have chopped you up, Will. I would have made you into a vampire, at the least." She swept out of the room in a cloud of sweet-smelling perfume.

I stared after her, aghast. She had left her half-filled glass on the counter, and it only took a bit of concentration to go solid long enough to lift the glass and sniff the contents.

Blood. So Maeve was a vampire? What other supernatural creatures roamed the streets of the city? Werewolves? Zombies?

"You're a vampire?" I finally asked when she reappeared dressed in more sedate attire.

Maeve smiled broadly enough for me to see her fangs. "Is that a problem?"

"No, not at all." Lysander *had* mentioned vampires, now that I thought about it. I concentrated, and held out my arm for the phoenix. It gave me a dubious look, then transferred itself to my wrist.

"I'll hold it if you want me to," Maeve offered. I think her offer was genuine, but the phoenix didn't want anything to do with it.

And, on reflection, neither did I. Staying solid for this long was good practice, after all. And I needed all the practice I could get.

Chapter 10

With the phoenix attached to my arm, I couldn't use my anchor to reach the cemetery, so I had to ride in Maeve's red Corvette. The phoenix wasn't very impressed. I was, but I think I managed to play it cool well enough.

Lysander met us at the gate. He stepped back when he saw Maeve, gawked at the phoenix on my arm, and led us to his grave without a word. Marla vanished when we walked past. Maeve didn't seem to notice.

Vampire strength was not misreported in the stories. Maeve grabbed the only shovel and got to work. By ten, Lysander's grave lay open to the night sky.

I felt like I should be helping, but the phoenix had eaten all my strength. I had finally persuaded it to perch on a tombstone, but it muttered darkly to itself as I tried not to let weariness drag me down into darkness. Lysander *had* claimed we no longer needed to sleep, but I felt refreshed and renewed after a good night's sleep. My mind still fancied it was alive instead of buried along the side of some godforsaken highway.

Maeve had to break the coffin lid to open it. The body inside had rotted away, leaving a skeleton behind.

Maeve straddled the grave and glanced up at me. "He only needs one bone?"

"Yeah. Is there any chance you can drop it off near the hospital?" The exhumation had upset Lysander. I didn't blame him. The thought of my own arm rotting away in someone else's crypt was bad enough. Mutilating his own body so he could be with Greta seemed only marginally stranger in comparison.

Without a qualm, Maeve reached down and picked up a tiny finger bone. "This should do it. Will? Are you coming with me?"

"I have to listen to your proposal, don't I?" I tried to keep my voice light, but I was too tired to pretend anymore.

"Thank you," Lysander said as I slid into Maeve's car, the phoenix back on my wrist.

"You're welcome," I said, just as gravely. "I hope..."

For one short second, Lysander looked like he was about to cry. Then he stiffened, and shook his head. "I know. Thanks, son. I owe you one."

I shook my head. "I'm just paying you back. Give us twenty minutes, then see if it works."

He could have come with us, I suppose, but neither Maeve nor I thought of that, and Lysander seemed to understand that we wanted to be alone. We dropped the finger bone in a flowerbed in front of the hospital, and returned to Rose's house. When Maeve pulled in the driveway, Rose ran out, gripping a bright blue feather in one hand.

"Maeve! Look what I found!" Her face froze when she saw me, then flushed when she saw the phoenix on my arm. She turned on her sister and thrust the feather in Maeve's face before she could get out of the car. "What is this? How dare you bring him here! Do you know what he did to Justin?"

Maeve pushed her sister away and climbed out of the car. Rose fell back, overbalanced, and landed on her rump in a plot of early pansies. I had to bite the insides of my cheek so I wouldn't laugh. Gallantly, or so I thought, I managed to go solid enough to offer her a hand, but she ignored me and struggled to her feet by herself.

"That man," she pointed at me with a shaking finger. "That man almost killed Justin, Maeve."

"*Justin* fashioned some sort of ghost trap," I said before Maeve could speak. "I persuaded him to let me go. I swore to him I'd come back and talk with you." I bowed as well as I could with a phoenix on my arm. "And here I am."

Rose lowered her hand. "That's exactly what Justin said. I thought he was lying."

"I have a feeling that Justin rarely lies," I said. "He seems to be a very well-rounded young man."

The last of Rose's fit of temper melted away. She ventured a small smile in my direction. "You found the phoenix."

"The phoenix found me," I said. "I'd really like to know what has been going on. Can we talk? Without exorcisms?"

Rose flushed. "I'm...I'm sorry about that. I tend to overreact where Justin is involved."

I bit my tongue and simply nodded.

Maeve sighed. "Shall we, then? *Some* of us only have until dawn."

So, with a tentative truce on the table, we followed her into the house.

Chapter 11

Justin sat at the kitchen table, still pale, but his eyes were lively enough when he saw the phoenix. "You found it!"

Before I could reply, the phoenix launched itself from my arm and flew over to him. It landed right in front of his glass of chocolate milk and inspected him carefully. Then it glanced back at me and chirped.

I had no idea what it was trying to tell me.

Maeve paid it no mind. She stuck the feather in a teacup and watched it burn with an intensity that would have frightened me had I still been alive. Rose vanished into the recesses of the house and returned a moment later in a pair of sweatpants and an oversized denim shirt. She had pulled her hair up into a messy bun. Compared to Maeve, she was only pretty, but I almost liked looking at her better. Rose was more...real. Maeve's ungodly beauty had to stem from the fact that she was one of the Undead.

"So, do we get to proposals now, or explanations?" I asked. "I'd really like to know what's going on."

Maeve turned around, opening her mouth to speak, but Rose beat her to it.

"Sheridan O'Rourke is our father," she said. "He's been tracking the phoenix's flight for years. It was due to land in the city three nights ago at the end of its cycle, and it did. But you saw it first."

"I still don't understand about that," I admitted.

Maeve pulled out a chair and motioned to it. "Sit down, Will. We won't...bite." She gave me a suggestive smile. I looked away only because the phoenix was glaring at me again.

I sat down. Maeve sat next to Justin, closer to the phoenix than I liked, but I didn't think she would double-cross me to get it. And if this 'guardian' thing were right, she wouldn't be able to do anything with it unless I was completely and utterly dead.

An exorcism would work, in that case. I glanced at Rose, but she didn't seem to be packing any holy water.

"Let me see if I can explain," Maeve said. "I've read the book; Rose hasn't."

"*I* don't hold an exalted position inside Sheridan's compound," Rose muttered darkly. I almost asked her what she meant by that, but decided to wait until later. I wanted to know about the guardian thing first.

"Every century, a phoenix is born and a phoenix dies," Maeve said. "The records aren't exact; some phoenixes were never recorded, so we're not working from a complete set of numbers. As far as we've been able to figure out, though, once every hundred years the old phoenix dies and is replaced by the new phoenix."

"That's in the books," I said. "Not the hundred years part; the legends weren't that exact, but that there is only one at any given time."

"Exactly." Maeve drummed her long nails on the table for a moment and stared at the phoenix. It seemed to be in some sort of staring match with Justin, but I didn't feel like interrupting.

"The guardians are the first person to see the phoenix when it arrives at a certain location. As far as we've been able to tell, each guardian is blessed by extraordinary wealth and power. When the phoenix moves on, which happens every ten years or so, the guardian is rewarded even further. Quite a few kings were guardians at one point. One of our Presidents was one." She paused. "Not all of the guardians have been good people, but the phoenix doesn't seem to be able to choose." The phoenix chirped in what sounded like agreement.

"And if the guardian dies?" Since this had happened to me, I felt like I had a good reason to ask.

"If the guardian dies, the next person to see the phoenix assumes the position," Maeve said. "That is why you were killed. I apologize for cutting up your body, but I didn't want the police to investigate."

Did she want me to accept her apology? To tell her it was okay? I nodded, not wanting to put my thoughts into words.

"Sheridan intended to be the phoenix's guardian ever since he pinpointed the date on which it would arrive in the city. As far as we can tell, it is at the end of its cycle, and the guardians at those times have been...very powerful indeed." She stared in disgust at the kitchen table.

I almost laughed. The phoenix, proving itself to be a true bird, had crapped right on the table.

Without a word, Rose cleaned up the mess and sat back down. She seemed, subdued, almost, as if she no longer knew what to do now that the phoenix was no longer lost.

"I think I have a fairly large birdcage in the basement, Will." She glanced at me. "Do you think the phoenix would mind?"

"I think if you set it up in the living room and left the door open, we could let it make up its own mind," I said.

Rose left to get the cage.

"If it shits on the carpet, I'll..." Maeve began.

At the end of the table, Justin stirred. "Aunt Maeve, you haven't finished your story yet." He hadn't been doing any magic that I could see, but his eyes were glazed and the circles under them were more pronounced. It was after midnight, after all, and the poor kid had been up far too late.

"Justin, if you want to go to bed..." I began.

He shook his head and sat up straighter. "I'm not tired." I truly doubted that, but I didn't want to argue with him. He wasn't my responsibility, after all.

"So, where does that leave us?" I asked. "I'm the guardian, I'm not all the way dead..."

Maeve waited until Rose had rejoined us at the table before she continued. The cage stood in the living room, a monstrosity of curly wire and peeling paint. The phoenix stared at it for a moment, glanced back at me with a look of disgust and flew into the other room. It inspected the cage for a moment, then huddled on the perch, its eyes closed.

"Well, that was easy enough," Maeve muttered. "Where was I?"

"If the guardian dies, the next person who sees the phoenix gets to be the guardian," Justin said, as if by rote. He didn't sound very happy about it.

"Oh, yeah." She glanced at me, then at her nephew. "Every once in a while, a war is fought over a phoenix. But that hasn't happened in a long time."

"What does Sheridan want with it?" I asked. "Money and power?"

"More money and power," Rose muttered. She, too, seemed uneasy. They all seemed to be waiting for something, but I had no idea what it was.

Maeve picked at the edge of the table. Rose twisted the hem of her shirt until I thought the fabric would tear. Justin propped his chin on his folded arms and stared across the table at me.

"So, what's your proposal?" I finally asked.

Maeve bit her lip. Rose sighed. Justin closed his eyes.

And someone knocked on the front door.

Rose and Justin reacted with identical expressions of terror. Maeve merely pushed her chair back and stalked out of the room, towards the phoenix.

I jumped up. "Hey, wait a second!"

Maeve didn't look back. "I *refuse* to let him have it." She lifted the cage with no apparent effort and vanished into the other room.

The person on the other side of the door knocked again, rattling the doorframe. Justin glanced at Rose, who reluctantly stood.

"I guess I'd better let him in."

He turned out to be the infamous Sheridan O'Rourke. From Marla's description of him, I had no trouble identifying him at all.

He reminded me of a rich CEO or perhaps a loan officer at a bank, not a bloodthirsty monster who would do anything for power. Alive, I wouldn't have trusted him within an inch of my throat. Dead, I faded through the nearest wall and ended up in the kitchen again.

"Sheridan." Rose's voice shivered. "What brings you here so late?"

"I can't pay a visit to my lovely daughter?" His false heartiness set my teeth on edge.

"It's almost one a.m.," Justin said, with only slight reproach in his voice. "We were...we were about to go to bed."

I heard movement from the other room, but didn't dare peek around the corner. No one had said Sheridan could see ghosts, but if *both* his daughters could, I thought there might be a strong possibility that he could as well.

"Did I see Maeve's car outside?" Sheridan asked. "Where is she?"

"I have no idea." Rose spoke so fast her tongue almost tripped over the words. "We were just about to go to bed, Sheridan..."

I heard a muffled yelp, then silence. I waited, straining to hear any sign of movement from the other room.

"You know better than to speak to me that way, Rose." Sheridan's voice had lost all of its civility. "Where is Maeve?"

"I'm right here." I heard a door open, and the click of Maeve's heels across the hardwood floor. "Are you torturing Rose for a reason, Sheridan?"

Rose gasped in a breath. "Damn..."

Sheridan chuckled. "Don't make me punish you again, Rose."

I risked everything to peek around the corner. Rose knelt in front of Sheridan, nursing her arm and a rapidly swelling eye. Justin stood with his back to the kitchen, clutching a handheld computer with one white-knuckled fist. I think he would have attacked his grandfather if he had enough strength.

Maeve stood in the doorway leading to Justin's room and the rest of the bedrooms, I supposed, her arms on her hips.

And Brooklyn and Lyle stood in the open doorway behind Sheridan.

If I had been solid, I would have crashed into the kitchen table and made enough of a racket to wake the dead. I reeled back from the sight of my murderers, too panicked to realize I was beyond their reach. Short of holy water and a well-aimed exorcism, they couldn't hurt me anymore.

It took me almost a full minute to gather up enough courage to approach the living room again. And this time, I was even less prepared when Sheridan himself walked right through me.

I got a confusing array of images from him, but couldn't make much sense out of them. But I had gained one important piece of information: Sheridan could not see ghosts. A moment later, when Brooklyn and Lyle joined him in the kitchen, I discovered that they couldn't see me either. That left only Maeve, Rose and Justin to spill the beans.

"I want to know what happened two nights ago," Sheridan said, and crossed to the patio door to peer out at the darkness. "Will Spark. Tell me about him."

Rose and Justin appeared in the doorway. Maeve brought up the rear. None of them glanced my way, but I saw Rose's shoulders tense.

"Why don't you ask your goons?" she snapped, showing a bit of spirit. "I had nothing to do with his death."

Sheridan didn't turn around to punish her again. He remained facing the sliding door, his expression lost in shadow. "Lyle, did you kill Mr. Spark like I instructed?"

"You bet, boss." Lyle smiled, reminiscing.

I didn't like the fact he was reminiscing about my murder, but there wasn't much I could do about it.

"If Will Spark is dead, then why hasn't the guardianship of the phoenix transferred to me?" Sheridan asked.

I had heard his tone of voice before. The man was *pissed*. I glanced at Rose and Justin and wondered if they realized how angry he was. I figured Maeve could take care of herself, being a vampire and all. I had a feeling she usually could.

"Maybe it's because you haven't *found* the phoenix yet?" Justin ventured to say.

Sheridan finally turned around. His smile did not reach his eyes. "Ah, yes. There is that *one* small detail. But weren't *you* supposed to be working on a computer program for me that would find the phoenix? Some sort of spell, Justin?"

Justin opened his mouth to respond, saw the expression on Rose's face, and wilted. "I'm not supposed to do that anymore," he whispered. "Not after...not after I was cursed."

"The phoenix holds the key to your curse, Justin." Sheridan's smile widened. "You know that. *I* know that. Your two lovely aunts know that." The last part was a warning aimed at Maeve. No one could have missed the look he gave her.

Maeve ignored both the look and his anger. "Justin's still recovering from the clean-up of Will Spark's apartment."

"There is no *time* for Justin to recover," Sheridan snapped each word off between his teeth. *"I want that phoenix found. Now."*

Rose snapped. "There's a reason why you can't be the phoenix's guardian," she whispered, not looking at me.

"And why is that?" Sheridan asked.

"Because Will Spark isn't all the way dead." Rose's voice cracked.

I couldn't really blame her for betraying me; she just wanted to protect her nephew. But her declaration *did* make my current position a bit more precarious.

"How could he not be all the way dead?" Lyle asked the obvious question. "Didn't you chop up his body, Maeve?"

"He's a ghost," Maeve said.

"A ghost." For the first time since he arrived, Sheridan looked a bit confused. "How can a ghost be a guardian?"

"I'm wondering the same thing myself," I whispered, content in the knowledge that he couldn't see me.

Justin gave the game away. When I spoke, he glanced towards me, and Sheridan finally realized what no one would come right out and say.

"He's *here?*"

Without an order from Sheridan, Brooklyn grabbed Rose and pressed a familiar switchblade against her neck. Justin started forward, but Sheridan grabbed him before he could try to rescue his aunt.

"Is he here? Now?"

Justin glanced at me and licked his lips. "Yes."

"What about the phoenix?" Sheridan almost drooled with thoughts of power. I had my doubts he would bother to break Justin's curse if he took control of the phoenix. He didn't seem to be the type.

"We didn't get a chance to find out," Maeve said smoothly. "He was about to tell us when *you* showed up."

"Justin, you know what to do." Sheridan nodded towards Brooklyn, who tightened his grip on Rose. "And you know what will happen if you refuse me."

Justin swallowed audibly. "But..."

Sheridan shook his head. "No buts."

Justin sighed and pulled a handheld computer out of his pocket. I tensed and reached out for an anchor, but I moved too late. Before I could say a word, he pressed a large button and I felt the familiar invisible bands constrict around me once more. I gasped when a ripple of pain forced me to my knees.

Sheridan squinted. "Ah. Mr. Spark, I presume?"

The bands around my chest tightened. I tried to draw in a breath, but managed only a gurgle.

Justin swayed. Sheridan caught his arm to steady him, but I didn't think he even noticed. The circles under his eyes--visible at the best of times--deepened and spread. Sweat beaded his brow.

I fought, even though I knew how badly it affected him. I did not want Sheridan to have control of the phoenix. I didn't want him to win.

"Rose?" Sheridan held out a small bottle. "You know what you have to do. If you hesitate, the spell will affect Justin even worse. I'll make sure of that."

A moment later, something wet flew through me and splattered the back of the kitchen cabinets. The holy water burned as it passed, leaving deep furrows of pain through my body. I tried to curl up on the floor in a desperate attempt to shelter myself, but I could not move.

I glanced at Rose when she began to speak the Latin phrases, and saw that she had tears running down her cheeks. Justin's eyes were suspiciously bright as well. And Maeve...

The last thing I saw before I fell away into darkness was Maeve's exit from the kitchen, and I realized what she had planned to do all along. Maeve didn't want Sheridan to have the phoenix either. She wanted it for herself.

But before I could warn Rose or Justin, the blackness swept me away.

Chapter 12

When I opened my eyes, I found I stood back in my apartment, in front of my bedroom mirror. Although I could see the mirror, I couldn't see my reflection in it at all. The effect was disconcerting, to say the least.

The holy water still hurt a bit when I moved, but I thought I could live with the pain. I walked out of the bedroom and into the living room, then stopped in the doorway to the kitchen. The apartment was still immaculately clean, but I could not look away from the spot I had died. I walked over to it, counting the tiles until I thought I was in the right place, but I hesitated to step inside the actual perimeters. I backed away.

The flashing light on the answering machine caught my eye, and I walked over to the phone. When I tried to go solid to punch the play button, nothing happened. When I tried to pick up the phone, my hand went right through it.

I stared down at the phone in dawning horror. Was *this* what it meant to be exorcised? I tried to find the pull of my anchors, but I felt absolutely nothing. My heart sank.

I drifted over to the front door, hesitated, then passed through it. When I opened my eyes, I was back in my bedroom again.

I don't know how much time passed while I tried to get out of my apartment. I passed through each and every window, went down every drain, and was heartily sick of my bedroom by the time I gave up. I couldn't even watch TV. I lay back on my bed, closed my eyes, and tried to fall asleep.

Late that night, something woke me. At first, I thought it was a dream. I opened my eyes and saw Justin standing at the foot of my bed, his eyes haunted by an unimaginable sorrow. I rose from my bed and followed him out of the room. He stopped in the kitchen, turned to stare at me, then quietly faded through the front door. When I tried to follow him, I found myself back in my bedroom again.

Had I been dreaming? Was Justin dead? I realized I had no way to find out, but that didn't stop me from being frustrated about it. I didn't want to spend the rest of eternity haunting my apartment. No wonder why most hauntings seemed to be so violent. I'd be violent too, if I was trapped in the same small space for hundreds or thousands of years.

Thinking about hauntings made me realize that even the most powerless ghost could affect inanimate objects. The ghosts in *Poltergeist* had been able to turn on the TV. Why couldn't I? They hadn't been exorcised, but then again, they seemed to be tied to one place.

Of course, I knew full well that *Poltergeist* was a movie, and therefore suspect, but I didn't have anyone to ask. I had to find out for myself.

With renewed vigor, I stood over the answering machine and stared at the play button. I lowered my finger to the button, concentrated with all my heart and soul, and pushed down.

Click.

"Hi, sorry I can't come to the phone right now. Leave a message and I'll get back with you as soon as I can."

"Will?" Rose's voice erupted from the speaker. "Will, I'm so sorry. I had to do it." She sounded like she'd been crying. "Justin's only fourteen."

I couldn't find it in my heart to blame her for betrayal. Sheridan seemed to have them all running scared. *All but Maeve.* I wondered if she'd become the phoenix's guardian already, or had Sheridan realized what she meant to do?

And had Justin been saved? Seeing his ghost did not bode well for their success.

"That was the only way to...to save his life. I'm so sorry." She hung up.

Did she truly know what she had done? I experimented with knocking the phone off the hook, then realized I could merely press another button. The hum of the dial tone filled the air.

It took me almost thirty minutes to summon up enough strength to press the buttons of Rose's phone number, and I had to start over twice because the stupid phone company decided I was taking too long. By the time I heard a ring on the other end, my vision was rimmed in black and I felt dangerously close to fainting.

The summons began before the second ring had ended. I felt something grab my soul and pull, much harder than my anchors had pulled me to them. I heard someone pick up on the line, but they only had a diminishing scream to answer their puzzled hello.

Chapter 13

Summonings hurt. I couldn't move for a full minute and I writhed in agony for a moment more before the pain wore off and I could see again. And when I saw who stared at me from outside the circle, I wished I could have stayed in agony for a little while longer.

An elderly priest goggled at me over an ancient prayer book. Rose stood beside him, equally frightened, her eyes bright with tears. Maeve stood on my right and Justin...Justin lay on the floor against the wall, his eyes closed. I didn't think he was breathing. I didn't see the phoenix or Sheridan anywhere.

I folded my arms and waited, but when no one seemed to want to break the silence, I sighed.

"You couldn't leave well enough alone, could you?" I'd read enough horror novels to know that I probably couldn't step across the boundaries of the circle, so I didn't even try. "Justin was right. I was in the wrong place at the right time, and my life has been hell ever since." The priest backed away from the circle. I turned to face Maeve. "Let me guess. Your plan didn't work?"

Maeve's mouth twisted. "Rose neglected to tell me that she had no true idea how to exorcise a ghost."

"Justin's dead, Will." Rose's voice cracked at the proclamation. "He's dead because you wouldn't die like you were supposed to."

I thought I detected a hint of life from the body, a movement or something, but I couldn't be sure. I held my tongue.

"Did you ever think I might have given up the guardianship if you had told me what you wanted?" I asked. "I never wanted to be involved in this. Justin was a nice kid."

"That doesn't matter now," Maeve said. "What matters is that you die truly now, so that I might assume the guardianship." She motioned to the priest. "No offense, Will, but I can't allow you to stand in my way."

"Just like you couldn't let Sheridan stand in your way?" I asked. "What did you do to him?" I felt no fear. In fact, I felt only helpless anger, as if fury was the only emotion I had room for in my heart.

Maeve licked her lips. "I did try to persuade him to see things my way before he died."

The priest stared at her in horror.

I almost felt sorry for him. "So, what are you going to do, then? Try to exorcise me again?"

"We're going to do it right this time," Maeve said. "Right, Rose?"

Rose opened her mouth to reply, glanced at Justin, and swallowed her words.

"All you have to do is tell me where the phoenix is, and then we'll get on with things," Maeve said, all business-like.

"What do you mean, *where's the phoenix?*" I stared at her. "*You* took it into the other room right before Sheridan showed up."

"And *you* slipped through the walls and released it," Maeve said. "I know you did. Where did you stash it, Will?"

"I didn't stash it anywhere," I said. I doubted she would believe me, but I didn't see any reason to lie. "After Rose and Justin performed their wonderful betrayal," Rose winced at this, "I found myself back in my apartment. I couldn't leave, and I didn't see a single phoenix. It took me hours just to dial the damned phone."

"I don't believe you," Maeve said. "You're holding out on me."

I spread my hands. "How? Whatever Rose did to me *hurt*. I was in no shape to go traipsing about the city unlocking birdcages."

At that moment, I could have cared less about the phoenix. If I hadn't gone to Larry's party, gotten drunk, and had to walk home, none of this would have ever happened. I would have been asleep in my own bed right now. I would have been *alive*.

"He can't lie in the circle," Rose whispered.

Oh, damn. I couldn't?

"What's your full name?" Maeve snapped.

I struggled to lie, but the words would not come out. "William Nathaniel Spark."

"Where is the phoenix?"

"I don't know."

"Why did Justin have to die?" Rose asked forlornly.

"He's not..." One of Justin's hands clenched into a fist. It was more of a spasm than a representation of anger, but I thought that was a good thing. "He's not dead."

Rose choked back a cry and ran to him. The priest stared down at Justin, then back at me.

"He *was* dead," he murmured. "I should know."

Maeve smiled and patted him on the hand. "Yes, you should know, Father. Were you responsible for this, Will Spark?"

Was I responsible? Did she think I was some sort of miracle worker? "No."

The priest glared at me, as if he suspected I was a demon instead of a ghost. "Are you certain?"

I smiled sweetly at him. "No."

The priest raised his prayer book. I guess I didn't react the way I was supposed to; I was too interested in Rose and Justin.

"He hasn't been breathing since early this evening. You show up and he's suddenly alive again?" The priest waved his book and stalked to the very edge of the circle. "I don't believe in coincidences."

"I didn't used to," I said. I had to admit it was a pretty large one to swallow, but if I had done something to bring Justin back, I had no idea what it was.

Justin moaned. He had four sets of eyes on him when he opened his own, and he winced away from the glow of the only lamp in the room.

"Justin? Can you hear me?" Rose's voice wobbled.

I cast a sidelong glance at Maeve. Had she done something to him to force him back?

Rose gasped. She had rolled Justin over, and we all saw the neat fang marks on his neck, the unmistakable mark of the vampire.

The priest looked from me to Maeve, then back to Rose and Justin. "Exactly *what* is going on here? I thought I was brought in to exorcise a ghost."

"You were." Maeve's voice did not waver.

"But the boy..."

"Just do your job, Father, and everything will be fine." Maeve walked away from the circle for the first time and stopped a few feet away from Rose and Justin. "You wanted him to live, didn't you?" She shrugged. "That was the only way."

Rose gathered Justin up into her arms. He didn't fight her, but lay like a broken doll in her embrace, his eyes dazed and unseeing. Would Maeve have done the same thing to me? I thought I'd much prefer being dead.

"I'm leaving." Rose's voice was perfectly calm, belying the hate in her eyes. "I'm leaving, and I'm taking Justin with me."

"I don't think so, Rose." Maeve shook her head. "I might need your...expertise. If this exorcism doesn't work..."

Rose had two choices: try to find another way past her sister or break the circle. She met my eyes, judged me in an instant, and stepped across the barrier.

The flash of light left me blind and hurled me somewhere else. I felt something slam into my body, felt something else squeeze my soul until I could do nothing but scream, and then the darkness again, rushing in to fill the void of consciousness.

Chapter 14

When the pain receded and I opened my eyes, I found I still lay in the basement room. The circle lay broken and smoldering on the floor, and the entire room was filled with smoke. The elderly priest, Rose, and Maeve were gone. Justin lay in a heap at the edge of the circle, his eyes closed.

I sat up and started to inspect my body for cuts and bruises before I realized it didn't really matter.

"They left me here," Justin whispered. "The...the priest said you were gone." He did not open his eyes.

"I don't understand why I'm still here," I admitted. "Shouldn't I have ended back in my apartment or something?"

Justin moved one hand and dug into the pocket of his jeans. Sealed inside a plastic bag were the scattered bones of what looked like a finger, or maybe a toe. I'd never been much for anatomy.

"I have one of your anchors," Justin whispered.

"My anchors didn't work after Rose did her thing," I said. "I couldn't get out of my apartment."

"Holy water will do that to you," Justin said. He concentrated and managed to prop himself up against the wall. The circles under his eyes were almost deep enough to drown in. I didn't see his glasses anywhere. "You just had to...recover."

"Did they lock you in?" I asked. I assumed I could escape with ease, providing they didn't have some sort of booby trap set for unsuspecting ghosts.

"I think so." Justin fumbled in another pocket and pulled out the little handheld. He stared at it for a moment, then sighed and set it on the floor. "Broken."

"Are you going to be okay?" I asked. What did one say to a newly born vampire? Congratulations?

"I'll be fine," Justin whispered. He closed his eyes. "I can't help you escape."

"I think I can handle it. I'm a ghost, remember?"

"There might be traps," Justin whispered. "If the computer worked, I could check, but..."

"I'll have to take that chance." I stood, feeling only a little wobbly around the edges.

"Rose didn't want to do that to you," Justin whispered. "She's really a good person. Maeve...Maeve wants the phoenix for herself."

"I gathered that," I said. "That's why she made a beeline to the birdcage when you and Rose tried to get rid of me."

Justin opened his eyes. "Yeah. But the phoenix was gone by then."

"I don't expect you had anything to do with that?"

Justin's mouth twisted. "I have the entire house rigged with my computer. I can affect anything."

So, he had trapped me and freed the phoenix in exchange for his life. I stared at him. "I'm not sure what to say."

"I didn't want to do that to you," Justin whispered. "You have to believe me."

I *did* believe him, but I also didn't want to consider trusting him anytime soon. "I believe you."

Justin did not look convinced. "Sheridan has...had been planning this for years." He coughed and wiped bright blood from his lips. "That's why he had Maeve made into a vampire. He intended to have her make him into a vampire once he had control of the phoenix."

"But Maeve didn't cooperate," I guessed. "And I assume Sheridan didn't think much of her plan to steal the phoenix from him."

"I think his body's still upstairs." Justin gritted his teeth and managed to stagger to his feet. "And now...now...I don't know what to do."

He sounded so...forlorn that I immediately went to him. I wasn't quite steady on my feet and neither was he, but I managed to stay solid long enough to reach a battered couch. He sank down with a sigh and closed his eyes.

I remained standing. The quicker I got out of the house the quicker I could find the phoenix and figure out what to do next. I wondered if Lysander had moved on, or if Greta was still fighting a losing battle. I wondered if I would ever see him again.

Wondering wouldn't help me get out of this mess. "Do you know where the phoenix is?"

Justin smiled. "I thought you'd never ask. Check in the laundry room. I locked the door, but the key's under the mat."

When I opened the door, the phoenix gave me a reproachful glance from on top of an ancient washing machine and chirped. I think it was happy to see me.

"If you bring my computer to me, I might be able to deactivate any traps," Justin whispered.

"I'm going to make a safe bet that they left too quickly to set any of your traps," I said, and passed through the basement door. I turned the key; left the door opened behind me, and explored the entire house before I felt safe enough to let the phoenix out of the laundry room.

It flew directly to the banana holder and perched there, glowering. I ignored it, helped Justin up the stairs, and poured him a glass of Maeve's drink. He was considerably stronger when the cup was empty. I, on the other hand, could have used about twelve more hours of sleep.

"So, what are you going to do now?" Justin sat behind his computer screen, doing something with a tracking program, or so he claimed. I suppose he could have been setting up another way to trap me, but I was growing rather tired of betrayals. *I* was the innocent in this, after all. I was the one who had been 'in the wrong place at the right time'.

"I'm not sure," I replied. "I have what they want, but what do they have that *I* want? They certainly can't bring me back to life."

"That's true." Justin tapped at a few keys and frowned. "I'm not picking up any of them at all. Do you suppose..." He shook his head. "I don't know what's wrong with it."

"Can I see?" I hovered over his shoulder while he gave me a rundown of his particular brand of magic. I was impressed in spite of myself.

"I should be able to find them using this, but I can't." He traced his finger across the screen and tapped it on a little blinking light. "This is Aunt Rose's house here. There should be more lights, but it doesn't seem to be working."

I sat back down. "Could that be a cause of your...condition?"

Justin's lips twitched. "My condition? I'm not sick anymore. I think Aunt Maeve broke the curse." He tapped a few more keys. "I...I think I'll miss the sunlight most of all." I looked away when he wiped his eyes.

"Tell me about your aunts," I said when he had regained his composure.

Justin sighed. "Maeve and Rose took me in when my parents were killed in an auto accident. I didn't know Maeve was a vampire until two years ago. They kept it a secret all that time." He sighed. "And Rose...Rose has always been a bit strange, but she's usually nice."

"What about your curse?" I asked. "What does that have to do with your aunts?"

"Nothing," Justin said. "The curse was my own fault. I did something I wasn't supposed to, and that was the result." He shut the computer too quickly and caught the side of his thumb in the latch. He hissed in pain.

I saw that his eyeteeth had grown. How would a fourteen-year-old boy live as a vampire? Unchanging, undying...if I had been made into a vampire when I was fourteen, I thought I would have killed myself by then. Fourteen was much too young for eternal life. At that moment, I hated Maeve and Sheridan so fiercely that the strength of that emotion surprised me. I didn't want them to have the phoenix or this boy.

"Can we presume Rose didn't go with them willingly?" I asked. I couldn't sit still, so I paced the kitchen floor, back and forth, past the phoenix until it reached out and tried to nip my arm. "Hey!"

It squawked at me and flew back into the living room where Maeve had left the empty cage. I watched it settle down on the perch, then turned back to Justin. "What do you think?"

"She didn't want to go," Justin said, chewing on his lower lip.

"Do you think they would hurt her?"

"Maeve really wants the phoenix," Justin said softly. He opened the computer back up and turned it on. "I'm going to try again."

We sat in silence for a little while as he chased glowing dots across his computer screen. "Hey! I think I might have something here..."

Before I could get up to look, the feather Rose had found burst into flames. They weren't ordinary phoenix flames. The teacup instantly melted into a jagged hunk of slag and the fire burned straight through the countertop in a matter of seconds. By the time I had a chance to blink, the entire cabinet was on fire.

"Fire extinguisher!" Justin erupted out of his chair, pulled the fire extinguisher out of its place beside the microwave, and let it fly. Thank goodness he had better reflexes than I did. He lowered the nozzle and stared at me. "What was that about?"

"I have no idea," I said, thinking of the feather in the pickle jar. Had it burst into flames too? Was my apartment building about to burn down? I felt like I should call someone with a warning, but they wouldn't have been able to hear me.

The world seemed to take a deep breath between the chink of cooling glass and the stench of burned Formica. I stared at the mess for a moment and wondered what Rose would say when she found out.

A second later, the phoenix itself ignited. So did the drapes. And the couch. And the coffee table. Justin managed to put out the fire before the house burned down around our ears, but it was a close call.

Chapter 15

If I had been alive, I would have offered Justin a beer, underage be damned. But we settled for relieved laughs as soon as the fire died, although Justin's smile faded as soon as he saw the charred lump of the birdcage in the middle of the mess.

I drifted over to have a look. The phoenix was gone, but it had left something behind.

"We don't have a phoenix anymore," Justin said. He tried to wipe the soot off his face and only made it worse.

"No." I concentrated, reached through the melted bars of the birdcage, and lifted the egg. It felt slick and heavy in my hand. "We don't have a phoenix. We have a phoenix egg." I didn't trust myself, so I lowered the egg back in its pile of ash. "Do you have any idea at all how long it takes a phoenix egg to hatch?"

"I have no..."

The phone rang, startling both of us. I was closer, so I picked it up. The plastic had melted a bit from the heat, but the phone still seemed to work.

"Maeve told me to tell you that she'll trade the phoenix for Rose," a familiar voice said in my ear.

"Lyle! It's been, what, almost four days since you murdered me?" I wondered if he could hear me. Lyle hadn't impressed me as much of a psychic, but I *had* learned quite a bit since then.

"Did you hear me? Maeve..."

"Maeve would hold her own sister hostage to get a bad-tempered bird?" I asked for Justin's benefit. He vanished into the other room, presumably to pick up an extension.

"Not..."

I heard a clatter, as if he had dropped the phone. Someone cursed. I waited patiently for them to get their act together.

"Will?" Rose's panicked voice reached my ear, but she wasn't anywhere near the phone. "Will, give them the damn bird!" I heard the sound of a slap, then sobbing in the background.

Someone else picked up the phone.

"Do you have the phoenix?" Maeve asked.

"Not exactly," I admitted. "What did you do to Rose?"

"The same thing I'd do to you if you were alive." Her voice was almost as cold as Rose's had been in the library. "I want the phoenix, Will. I'll trade Rose for the bird."

"I'd trade you if I had it," I said. "But..."

"Aunt Maeve? Why are you doing this?" Justin sounded as if he was crying.

Maeve was quiet for a long time. I thought I heard Rose say something in the silence, but I couldn't make out the words. "Justin, you're too young to understand."

"I'll always be too young, won't I?" Justin asked. "Because of what *you* did to me."

"I didn't want you to die." Maeve's voice softened. "I don't care what they say about me; you'll always be my favorite nephew."

I had no idea how Justin would react to that. If I was in his shoes, I would have slammed down the phone and refused to speak to her again, but he had been raised by his aunts. He had trusted them, and Maeve, at least, had betrayed him.

"Do you have the phoenix?" Maeve asked when Justin didn't reply to her proclamation.

"Not exactly," I hedged.

"What is that supposed to mean? Either you have it or you don't."

"We *did* have it," I said, staring at the white egg nestled in the pile of gray ash. "Except..."

"It burned, didn't it?" Maeve's voice dropped. "Damn you, Will Spark!"

"Hey, I had nothing to do with that," I hastened to assure her. "Tell Rose the house is fine, but she'll need a new living room and a new kitchen cabinet. If it's any consolation, my apartment is probably burning down as we speak." The TV was in the living room, covered in white foam from the fire extinguisher. Would the news show something as mundane as an apartment fire?

"Did it lay an egg?" Maeve demanded.

I sighed. "You know it did." She shouted something to someone, holding the phone away from her face so I couldn't hear what she had said.

"Listen, Will. This is the deal. In ten minutes, I'm going to have priests in every cemetery in the city. If you don't bring the egg and my nephew to me in thirty minutes, I'll exorcise every ghost in this godforsaken place."

I thought of Tim, and Marla, and the two little girls. And the countless others who I had not yet met. Rose's little banishing had not been close to a true exorcism, and that had *hurt*. I couldn't imagine what an actual exorcism would feel like.

"Where are you?" I asked. It was close to three a.m. Dawn was less than four hours off. I covered the mouthpiece with one hand.

"Justin?"

He appeared in the doorway, calm and composed. His eyes were a little red-rimmed from weeping, but I didn't comment on that.

"Will you go with me to rescue Rose?"

"I have to, don't I?"

"No. You don't. You could stay here and wait for me to come back."

"*If* you come back," he said.

"There is that." I indicated the egg. "Do you think you could find something safe to put that in?"

"We're down at the riverfront," Maeve said as soon as I put the phone back up to my ear. "In the park, near the shelter house. You shouldn't be able to miss us."

I remembered the horrible pull of the water and shuddered. I did not want to go near the river again, but I had no choice. If Maeve was serious, and I had no way to tell if she was or not, I'd have to give up the phoenix egg or Rose would die.

"If you bring my nephew and the egg to me, I'll let Rose go and never contact her again," Maeve said. "If you don't, I'll sprinkle her all over the city like I did to you."

"We'll bring it," I said, the bare bones of an idea slowly forming in my mind. The phoenix egg was just about the same size as an extra-large Grade A. Would Maeve be able to tell the difference if I replaced the phoenix egg with something else? Would she expect treachery from me? Did I dare even contemplate tricking her? One signal from Maeve and every cemetery in the city would be purged. Did I dare play with fire while I was responsible for the lives of so many ghosts?

As soon as I hung up the phone, I detailed Justin in on my plan. He seemed skeptical at first, but when I compared the phoenix egg to a chicken egg and couldn't find a difference, he warmed up to it enough to volunteer to bike the egg to the riverfront. That way, I could use one of my anchors to spy on Maeve before he arrived, and make sure she hadn't lied to us.

I thought it was a good plan. I didn't know how wrong I was.

Chapter 16

I used my left foot to get me close enough to the riverfront, intending to walk the rest of the way. I had seen Justin off with the chicken egg tucked securely in the basket of his bicycle. He didn't seem to think he would have a problem reaching the riverfront in less than thirty minutes, and I wasn't about to argue with him. I'd seen Maeve's strength when she dug up Lysander's grave, and I had no doubts that Justin now shared some of the same attributes.

My plan was simple and relied a lot on luck. I thought we had a good chance of pulling it off, but I didn't expect a reception when I arrived at my anchor. Lyle and Brooklyn had just rescued my foot from its shallow grave when I arrived. Being that I had no other anchors in the vicinity, I had no true choice but to follow them.

They carried my poor foot in a bait bucket, but they didn't look like fishermen at all. I have never seen a fisherman in a suit. I sat in the backseat of their car as they drove down the lonely road to the riverfront, and tried not to remember that I had allowed a fourteen-year-old to *bike* down here. Yes, he was a vampire, but I still didn't feel comfortable about it.

Lyle and Brooklyn didn't notice me at all. It would have been fun to torment them by turning off the headlights or making the radio tuner move by itself, but they might have gotten suspicious, and I didn't need another shot of holy water to send me on my way. We arrived at the park without incident or notice. I hadn't realized it before, but the whole riverfront district seemed to be completely deserted. Granted, it *was* three in the morning, but I always expected to see a bum or two.

Maeve stood under the only spotlight in front of the shelter house, her red hair flaming in the dimness. She wore a black halter-top and a skimpy pair of shorts. Her long legs shone like twin beacons of light.

I shook my head and looked away. I didn't need the phoenix to tell me she was up to no good; I knew already. I scouted around a bit for Rose, but I couldn't find her anywhere. Where had Maeve stashed her?

When I followed Maeve, Lyle, and Brooklyn into the shelter house, I got the shock of my life. Almost my entire body lay in pieces on one of the picnic tables, from severed head down to my little toe. I hadn't even felt them moving my anchors.

She'd missed a couple, like the finger in the gutter on Fourth Street and the arm from Lysander's cemetery, but the rest of my body was present and accounted for, in varying states of decay. I took care to stay out of her line of sight. I didn't want her to see me and give the game away.

"That's going to have to do," Maeve said. "We don't have enough time to find the rest of it. Do you have the bags?"

Bags? What did they need bags for? They needed an air freshener. If I had been alive, the stink would have bowled me over. Even Lyle and Brooklyn looked a bit green around the gills.

I watched as they loaded my body parts into fabric bags and loaded rocks in with them. They tied the bags closed with strong twine, picked up as many as they could carry, and took the whole stinking mess to a small rowboat bobbing in the dark water. I didn't realize what they meant to do with the bags until they dropped the first one overboard. Maeve stayed on shore, of course.

The nausea hit me like that semi had. I wavered and almost fell. Maeve turned, searching the darkness for me, I presume, and I ducked behind a garbage can and tried to hold onto my sanity. I felt the water seeping into the fabric bags. I felt each and every body part individually as they floated to the bottom of the river.

I think the rest of my anchors were the only things that saved me. I didn't vanish when the last one went overboard, but I felt as if I had been on a week-long drunk. I couldn't even stand; my legs were so weak. I watched as Lyle and Brooklyn anchored the boat and vanished into the darkness. I knew they were setting a trap, but I didn't have enough strength to warn Justin.

A few minutes later, I heard bike tires on the gravel parking lot. Before I could struggle to my feet to warn Justin, Lyle and Brooklyn attacked. Lyle took the bike and the lunch bag; Brooklyn held Justin in an unbreakable grip. Vampire or no, the kid *was* only fourteen. He put up a valiant struggle, but he couldn't fight a full-grown man.

Maeve appeared in the spotlight again. "Justin. Where's Will?"

"He's..." Justin looked around wildly, as if he expected me to appear out of the darkness and save him. I managed to get to my knees, strengthened, I think, by the finger bone Justin still had in his pocket, but I didn't dare leave the shelter of the garbage can yet.

"I see." Maeve approached them and ran one finger down the side of Justin's face. "I want you to do something for me, Justin. If he's here, we'll flush him out."

"What do you want me to do, Aunt Maeve?" He quivered at her touch.

"I want you to use your ghost trap to find him," Maeve said. "Did you bring your computer?"

"N...no." Justin tried to escape when she took his arm, but he was no match for her strength.

Maeve's lips tightened. "Not even your handheld?"

"It got broken when I..." Justin looked around for me one last time. "When I died, Aunt Maeve." His shoulders slumped.

I almost gave myself away, but what good would I have done then? I crouched behind my garbage can and tried to think of a plan. I needed to find Rose, first off. After Rose, then I had to figure out a way to rescue Justin from his aunt before she realized the phoenix egg was a fake. Perhaps my little deception had not been a good idea after all.

But first...I eyed Maeve's Corvette and wondered just how many wires I'd had to pull to disable it. It only took a moment for me to slip underneath and a moment more to grab whatever I could and pull those wires free. Some kind of fluid sprayed through my body, but I didn't care. It wasn't like my clothes were going to get dirty. There was a Porsche parked nearby as well, but I didn't have enough time to disable both cars. One would have to do.

After my little bit of sabotage, I scurried from garbage can to garbage can until I reached the shelter house again. Maeve had propelled Justin to the bloodstained and gore-encrusted picnic table. Lyle and Brooklyn stood on either side of him, preventing his escape.

The lunch bag sat in the middle of bits and pieces of my decaying flesh, looking very innocent in the midst of all that mess.

"Open the bag," Maeve said to Justin. "And tell me the truth. Did he keep his word?"

"Yes," Justin whispered. "He wanted to trick you, but I switched the eggs when he wasn't looking."

For a short, heart-stopping moment, I actually believed him. *Had* he switched the eggs? I remembered giving him the chicken egg to wrap up in a roll of paper towels, but he hadn't gone anywhere near the phoenix egg, had he?

I had no way to find out unless I asked him, and I didn't exactly have a good way to do so. I would have to hope and pray he was lying.

Justin opened the bag and drew out the wad of paper towels. He slowly began to unwrap the egg; drawing out the suspense until Maeve uttered an oath and grabbed it out of his hands. When the unassuming white egg lay exposed on the bed of paper towels, she stared at it for a minute, then drew a small pocketknife out of the pocket of her shorts. She pulled up the little knife and walked around the table to where Justin sat. Lyle and Brooklyn moved in to flank him.

Justin paled. "It's the real egg!"

Maeve drew one hand through his hair. "I really hate to do this to my favorite nephew, but I have to make sure you're telling me the truth, Justin. Wouldn't you agree?" She took his hand and laid it flat on the picnic table. "This knife is sterling silver. Do you know what silver does to vampires?"

Justin chose that moment to try to slide under the table. Lyle grabbed a handful of his hair and pulled him up. After that, they held him too tightly for him to move anything at all.

Maeve held the little knife over Justin's splayed hand, right between two of the larger bones. She pressed down, making a tiny dimple in his skin, and I saw a blister rise even from that little contact with the silver.

"This won't kill you, but it *will* hurt." She pushed the knife down. Brooklyn covered Justin's mouth with one meaty hand to block his scream. Justin writhed in their grasp.

Maeve pushed the knife all the way through his hand and into the table. She stepped back and watched him struggle for a little while until he realized he was just making it worse. When he finally quieted, she walked to the front of the table to face him.

Chapter 17

I chose that moment to play my nonexistent hand. I stepped out of the shadows long enough for Justin to see me, put one finger in front of my lips, and slipped away again, wanting to enter the shelter house from the other side. I heard a barge sound in the distance, but I didn't pay it any mind.

"Now tell me the truth, Justin," Maeve said as I slipped in the opposite end and hid myself in the shadows. "Is this the real egg?"

Justin had tears pouring down his cheeks, but he held to the fiction admirably. He nodded. Again, I wondered if he had really double-crossed me. Surely not, but I had no way to tell.

"If I tell Eddie to take his hand away from your mouth, I don't want to hear you scream. Do you understand? I promise you I won't hurt you anymore."

Another nod. So Brooklyn's name was Eddie? It fit. Eddie started to remove his hand, and Justin made his move. He must not have trusted Maeve. I didn't blame him. He bit down savagely on Eddie's hand, tearing out a chunk of flesh and leaving him with a gaping hole in his palm. Eddie jerked back and knocked into Lyle, who released Justin's other arm to catch himself so he wouldn't fall.

Justin jerked the knife from his hand and scuttled across the picnic table bench until he was up against the wall. He held the knife out in front of him, but with the blood running down his chin and the tears mixing in with the blood, he didn't look very menacing.

He gagged and forced himself to swallow. I winced and looked away. I couldn't imagine what human flesh tasted like, especially Eddie's, but it couldn't have been very palatable. Even to a vampire.

Throughout this spectacular escape, Maeve had not moved a muscle. When Justin stopped his mad rush along the rough wooden bench, she finally turned to regard him. Her eyes were hard and cold, her lips pressed into a thin line. She resembled my second sight of Rose so much that I had to blink and shake my head to push those memories back in their proper places.

Justin's hand shook so badly I feared he would drop the bloodstained knife, so I decided to throw caution to the winds and back him up. When I stepped out of the shadows to stand beside him, he visibly relaxed. Maeve, on the other hand, only laughed.

The barge sounded again. I'm not sure why that sound sent a ripple of fear through my body, but Justin noticed. Maeve did too.

"Did you find Rose while you were out lurking around? Or did you miss her? I'll give you a hint; she's hidden in plain sight."

"I didn't find her." *Had* I passed her by somehow? I hadn't seen any likely places to stash a full-grown woman, unless Maeve had put her on a boat out on the water...that thought stopped me cold. Hidden in plain sight? In a boat? On the water? With a barge on its way?

"Where is she, Maeve?" I asked. My voice sounded tinny and strange to my ears. I felt like I was about to faint. Again. I struggled past the feeling and concentrated on the task at hand. Rose. I had to find Rose.

"We couldn't let the extra rowboat go to waste," Maeve said, confirming my guess. "She's anchored out in the middle of the river, Will." She smiled just as sweetly as I had back in the basement. "And I thought I heard a barge coming. Whatever will you do?"

"Aunt Maeve!" Justin gasped.

"Is this the real phoenix egg?" Maeve asked, still smiling.

"No," I sighed.

"Yes," Justin said at the same time. We exchanged glances, but I couldn't read the expression on his face.

"Which is it? Yes or no? Tell me the truth and I'll send Lyle out to bring Rose back. Don't tell me the truth, and you can pick up the pieces as they are washed ashore." She glanced at her watch. "I'd say you have about eight minutes before that barge makes toothpicks out of the rowboat."

"It's real," Justin said. He cradled his bleeding hand against his chest. "I told you; Will didn't know." The circles were back under his eyes, but I saw no other sign of strain. Eddie's blood slowly dried on his face. *Had* he betrayed me?

"Bring her in," I whispered hoarsely. "Don't let her die out there."

Maeve finally seemed satisfied that Justin was telling the truth. She snatched up the egg, carefully rewrapped it, and stowed it away in the lunch bag. "Lyle, go bring my sister back."

Lyle left the shelter house. Eddie sat and glared at Justin, his wounded hand swathed in what looked like a scarf. Had it been Rose's? Would Lyle be too late? I pushed away from the wall, intending to follow him, but Justin stopped me.

"Don't go. Please, don't go." His eyes were losing focus fast, and the wound in his hand had not healed at all. The front of his shirt was wet with blood.

Maeve vanished into the night, presumably to check Lyle's status. She took the lunch bag with her. Eddie continued to glower, but I didn't think he could hear us if we kept our voices low.

"Was that really the phoenix egg in that bag?" I hissed.

Justin gave me a small, strained smile. "No, of course not. But she believed me. That's all that matters, isn't it?"

I heard Lyle shout something outside, and Maeve's furious reply. Justin was off the bench before I pushed myself away from the wall, and I followed him closely as he ran out into the night.

Eddie didn't try to stop us. I'm glad he didn't, neither Justin nor I were in any shape to fight him. Eddie couldn't see me anyway, so I guess it didn't really matter.

Chapter 18

Lyle stood at the edge of the water, staring after the drifting empty rowboat that had somehow broken loose of its moorings. He turned towards Maeve, who stood at the top of the sloping hill, his arms upraised. I could read his expression from where we stood.

And I realized I could see Rose's rowboat anchored out in the water, a dark shape bobbing on the river. I couldn't see Rose, but at least the rowboat was still intact.

Or would be, for another five minutes. I saw the barge emerge from around a bend in the river and start towards the rowboat. The horn sounded again. It wasn't going very fast, but even a slow barge would grind that little rowboat up and spit out the pieces.

"Rose! Rose, can you hear me?" Justin's voice barely carried to where Lyle stood.

"She's gagged, of course," Maeve said. "I didn't want her to yell for help." She held up the bag. "Unfortunately for you, Lyle let the rowboat slip. I think we'll be leaving now." She started towards her Corvette.

"Wait! You can't just leave her out there! She's your *sister*, Maeve!"

Maeve didn't turn around. She beckoned to her men, who climbed into the sleek Porsche. Eddie gave Justin a nasty look when he passed. Justin didn't notice. I didn't really want to let them go, but I didn't see that we had much of a choice. Neither Justin nor I would be much good in a fight.

I heard both cars start, both engines rev. Had I disabled the only set of wires that wouldn't do a thing?

The Porsche drove away in a squeal of rubber, but Maeve seemed to be having some sort of problem with the Corvette. I smiled, despite the situation.

"What are we going to do, Will?"

"I don't know." I had no desire to brave the river again, especially so soon after my anchors had been thrown into a watery grave. I followed him down to the edge of the river and stared out at the bobbing rowboat.

I heard Maeve curse and press on the gas. She shifted the car into gear, but it didn't go forward when she pressed on the gas. Instead, it jerked backwards, towards the river.

Justin tried to climb in, but he couldn't seem to push against the current. I don't know if it was his new nature or pure exhaustion, but he collapsed, gasping, on the bank. And the rowboat bobbed out in the middle of the river, waiting for the barge to crush it to pieces.

I watched as Maeve fought the steering wheel, struggling to turn the Corvette from its path. But I had done my job too well. The car zoomed backwards, hit a speed bump, and landed rear-first, into the river.

"I'll kill you!" Maeve screamed. She scrambled at the door of the Corvette, struggling to open it. But even though I hadn't done a thing about the locks, the door would not open.

Perhaps one of those wires had been for the electrical system.

The barge grew closer, oblivious to the rowboat that lay in its path. I doubted we could warn the pilot in time to change course or stop it. I took a deep breath I didn't need and saw that Justin still held Maeve's little knife in his hand.

"Give me the knife."

He stared at me. "You can't go into the water either, can you?" He alternated his gaze between the rowboat and Maeve's predicament with the Corvette. "Did you do something to her car?"

"I'm going to have to," I said. "You're not strong enough, and I'm not going to leave Rose to die. I'm going to try my best to free her." I glanced at Maeve, who was evidently attempting to claw through the roof of the car as it slid into the water even further. The front wheels caught on the speed bump. "What I want *you* to do is take care of your aunt. I think you know what to do."

Justin fished a sodden plastic bag out of his pants pocket and held it up. "I have your anchor," he whispered. He glanced at Maeve again. "And yes. I think I know what to do."

"One of the last anchors in existence," I told him. "Maeve had them throw most of my body in the river." I took the knife, closed it, and realized I would have to hold it; my pockets weren't really pockets anymore. I thought I'd have a better chance keeping my hand solid than a pocket anyway. "Wish me luck."

Justin swallowed and coughed. "Good luck."

I took another deep breath I didn't need, fixed the bobbing rowboat in my line of vision, and jumped into the river.

Chapter 19

The shock hit me like a physical blow. I held onto the pocketknife by willpower alone, knowing that if I dropped it, I might as well pull myself away to the safety of one of my anchors and leave Rose to die. I floundered in the water for a bit, unable to get my bearings, and then I saw the empty rowboat bobbing in the current ahead of me. I ignored it. I didn't have enough strength to row, and I doubted Rose would be in any shape to do anything but swim for her life.

I gritted my teeth and fought the pull of the water. It wanted to sweep me away; to send me fleeing back to land, but I couldn't leave Rose to die.

Each inch was an effort. The current felt like holy water passing through my body, leaving only agony behind. I gasped and spluttered and pushed every ounce of strength I had into my clenched fist, but I was beginning to think even that wouldn't be enough. I would drop the knife, it would fall straight down into the muck that covered the river floor, and Rose would die.

Sheer stubbornness kept me from giving up. I couldn't see the rowboat anymore; my sight had faded away with the last of my strength, but I heard the barge horn echo loudly across the water, and knew I was running out of time.

When my clenched fist touched wood, I didn't know what it was at first. I grappled with this new obstacle for a moment, blind and hurting from the waves, until I realized it was the anchored rowboat.

I had made it after all.

From somewhere, I found enough strength to pull myself into the boat. I lay there beside Rose for a moment and tried to put myself back together, but I had no strength left to fight the pull of the water. My sight slowly returned.

Rose stared at me with frightened eyes as I fumbled to give her the pocketknife. She didn't understand at first, but when she touched the cold silver of the blade, she tried her best to slice through her bonds.

The barge horn sounded again. Even in my weakened state I realized she would never get free and swim away in time. Either the barge would plow her under or she would be drowned by the wake. Justin couldn't help her; he stood on the bank, anxiously pacing at the edge of the water, too close to collapse to fight the water himself. He had risked his life to lie to Maeve, and died once already because of it. I didn't want to send him to a watery grave as well.

I saw no sign of Maeve's car. Justin had done well.

I lay on my back in the bottom of the boat and tried to push past the weariness that threatened to overcome me. I managed to reach over the side of the boat and feel for the rope that secured the anchor. Luck was with me; it wasn't a chain, but a rope, wet and slimy with rot.

"Give me the knife." I could barely hear my own voice.

Rose still struggled with her bonds. She quieted and let me take the pocketknife as soon as she realized what I meant to do, but I could see the doubt in her eyes. I wondered what I looked like to her. Was my form flickering like my vision was? Had I faded? Did I look like I was being tortured by the devil himself?

I gritted my teeth and funneled the rest of my strength into my hand, forcing it to stay solid no matter what. I had to cut the anchor rope, Rose's bonds, and then hope for the best. If we were lucky, the rowboat would drift enough on the current to miss the barge, or only be hit by a glancing blow. *If we were lucky.*

I felt the rope slip under my fingers, and tightened my grip on the knife. Every scrap of strength I had went into slicing through that rope, and when I finally felt it give under my fingers, my relief was so great that I almost dropped the knife.

I turned to Rose and cut through her bonds. She tore off the gag and untied her feet; her eyes fixed on the fast approaching barge. I could no longer see it. As soon as the last rope had split under the blade of the knife, I felt something crack against the side of the rowboat. The boat rocked wildly. I heard Rose scream my name, but I was already gone. The water sucked me down into darkness and bore me away.

Chapter 20

When I opened my eyes, I found I lay back on the crypt in the cemetery again, staring up at the maple trees that sheltered my arm's resting place. I lay there for a moment, weary in soul, if not body, and tried not to remember the water. And Rose.

The sun shone brightly overhead. I had no idea how much time had passed, but I doubted it had been more than a day...two at the most.

"Will? Are you awake?"

Tim stood at the foot of the crypt, dressed in his uniform. He held his cap under one arm, and his blond hair blew in the breeze that rustled through the trees above me.

"I'm awake." I was awake, but I had no desire to move. I felt as if my body was part of the granite, solid and sure, unmovable and far, far away from any bodies of water.

"Are you okay?"

I could still feel the path of the water through my body. Everything hurt, from each individual hair on my head to my toenails. I closed my eyes.

"If I said I'll live would you leave me alone?"

He laughed. "I'm not sure. What happened?"

Haltingly, I explained about Maeve, Rose, Justin, and the Phoenix. The telling took most of my limited amount of strength, and I drifted off for a little while afterwards, content to lay on the granite and soak up the strength of the sun.

When I next opened my eyes, Marla stood beside me. She drew on her cigarette and bent over my body. "Is Rose alive?"

That question seemed to be important, but I couldn't find the strength to care. I needed rest, and lots of it, before I could even begin to contemplate finding out if she had made it to safety.

"I don't know."

"Leave him alone, Marla," Tim appeared beside her, took her arm, and led her away. "He needs to rest."

But once Marla had asked the question, I couldn't seem to bring myself to forget it. I lay on the granite for another hour, then slowly pushed myself up. I swung my legs over the side and sat there for a little while, nausea swimming in my stomach.

"Are you sure you're going to make it?" Tim asked.

"I need to find out if they're alive," I whispered.

"You look like hell," Tim observed.

I managed to smile. "I feel worse. But I'll live, for want of a better word." When I stood, I had to grab the granite for support. "How long have I been here?"

"You appeared there late last night," Tim said. He glanced up at the sky. "It's about four o'clock now."

"No...sign of Rose or anyone?" I asked.

"No. The cemetery's been fairly quiet." He paused. "Greta died. Lysander moved on. He wanted me to thank you."

I would have shrugged, but it hurt too much. "I would have done that for anyone, especially Lysander. He was a nice guy."

"Yeah, he was." Tim got a faraway look on his face for a moment, and then snapped back to the present. "There was a priest here for a couple of hours last night, but he left right before you appeared."

I told him about Maeve's threats.

He paled. "*All* the cemeteries?"

"That's what she said. I didn't want to test out any theories, but at least she didn't get the phoenix egg." If Justin hadn't really pushed her car into the river, she could have easily gone back to Rose's house and taken it, and I realized I'd have to go there as well. But first, I'd visit the river and make sure Rose's lifeless body wasn't face down on the bank somewhere.

It took most of my strength to pull myself to the river, and my stomach churned just standing on the bank staring out at it. The remnants of the night before lay scattered in the calm water like the debris after a storm, scattered pieces of one of the rowboats lay strewn across the water. I found the plastic bag that held my finger bone lying on the concrete, and wondered if Justin had dropped it on purpose. I picked it up and used a little of my carefully hoarded strength to make my pocket solid enough to carry it. My hand still hurt from the previous night's ordeal.

The bloody picnic table looked even worse in daylight, but I didn't really care about that. I walked along the bank for almost a mile before I saw the other rowboat, seemingly undamaged; lying abandoned on a weedy patch of the riverbank.

I didn't see Maeve's car anywhere, but if it lay at the bottom of the river, I didn't expect to see it. How long would it take for the police to investigate? Would they realize the nasty fly-infested goop on the picnic table had once been human remains?

Dared I surmise by the position of the rowboat that someone had dragged it out of the water and that someone had been Rose? Justin wouldn't have been able to cross the water, but I could imagine them yelling across the river at each other until Rose clambered up the bank and crossed on one of the two bridges nearby. I could imagine it all I wanted to, but had it really happened?

To find out, I would have to go to Rose's house, but I didn't think I had enough strength to go anywhere I didn't have an anchor. I barely had enough strength to pull myself back to the cemetery, where I ignored Marla's shouted questions, lay down on my bed of granite again, and slept the rest of the day away.

Chapter 21

When I awoke, night had fallen and the patterns the maple leaves made across the full moon caught my attention until Tim cleared his throat.

"You have visitors."

Visitors? Plural? I pushed myself up and saw Justin first, slumped against a gravestone with his eyes closed. He had something nestled in his lap, but I couldn't tell what it was. Rose stood in deep conversation with Marla, who nudged her when she saw I was awake.

Rose turned around. Her face lit up when she saw me, and she shook Justin until he opened his eyes. The bundle in Justin's lap squawked. My heart sank.

A newborn phoenix is the ugliest animal on the planet. It was pink and almost featherless, with little tufts of what looked like white hair sticking out of its ears. Its beak was mottled blue and purple, and its eyes were black and shiny. It looked like a half plucked chicken.

"The egg hatched," Justin said.

I stared at the creature in his arms. It was much too large to have hatched out of that egg, but I didn't argue with him. I shook my head and transferred my gaze to Rose.

"What about Maeve?"

Justin bit his lip and glanced at Rose. "She's gone. I don't know what happens to vampires under water, but it can't be good."

Well, if Maeve was gone, that left Eddie and Lyle to take care of. Which shouldn't be difficult, all considering. I was well, non-living proof that it *was* possible to hide a body in the city. Certainly there was room enough for two.

"Hello, Will." Rose wasn't wearing the ugly coat or the horrid hat anymore. She wore a nice navy blue hooded sweatshirt, a pair of faded jeans, and running shoes. I couldn't see her shirt, but the jacket did nice things to her hair. At least *someone* had made it out of this mess alive.

"Hi." I had never been any good at small talk.

Justin rolled his eyes, gathered up the baby phoenix, and moved under a maple tree with Tim. Rose approached hesitantly, as if she expected me to order her away, but I had never been one to hold grudges.

"I think I owe you an apology," Rose began. "I was...misled. I shouldn't have trusted Maeve."

"I shouldn't have trusted her either," I admitted. "You weren't the only one at fault, you know." I patted the top of the crypt. "Why don't you sit down? You can't be very steady on your feet yet."

"I'm not." She took the seat gratefully, and I scooted over to give her enough room. "Justin told me most of the story, but I don't understand one thing."

"Just one?" I smiled at her. "I don't understand at least a half dozen still, and I doubt I ever will."

"That's probably true." Rose's eyes were suspiciously bright. She turned away and wiped her tears with a tissue. "I didn't think she'd hurt me. We grew up together!"

"Sometimes, the promise of power and wealth will turn even the most level head," I said slowly. "I think Maeve saw the phoenix as a way to get back at your father for doing what he did to her."

Rose shuddered. "I don't understand why you risked your life to come after me. Tim said you could have been killed!"

Why *had* I gone after her? She spoke the truth; even Lysander had warned me away from water, and I hadn't fully recovered yet. Why had I risked everything to save her life?

The moonlight played across her hair and lit it up like a beacon of fire. Her face looked both vulnerable and mysterious, as if I had disturbed some long-forgotten goddess out of sleep. I knew why I had risked everything to save her now. I reached out, turned her face towards mine, and kissed her.

I managed to stay solid until the phoenix landed in my lap. After that, we were laughing too hard for solidity to matter.

The end

You can find ALL our books up on our website at:

http://www.writers-exchange.com

All Jennifer's books:

http://www.writers-exchange.com/Jennifer-St-Clair/

all our fantasy novels:

http://www.writers-exchange.com/category/genres/fantasy/

About the Author

Jennifer St. Clair grew up in Southern Ohio and spent most of her childhood in the woods around her home. She wrote her first novel when she was thirteen, and hasn't stopped since. She lives with her ball python, Fester, and two cats, Ash and Rowan.

In her spare time, she crochets, makes cloth dolls, collects antiques, books, and vintage clothing, and takes digital photographs with varying degrees of success.

Her *Beth-Hill series* is set in the area in America that contains many supernatural creatures: Wild Hunt, Vampires, Dragons, Faery and more.

It is part of the Universe that her *Jacob Lane Series*, *Karen Montgomery Series* and vampire trilogy, *The Shadow Series* are set in.

Follow all her books on her author page:
http://www.writers-exchange.com/Jennifer-St-Clair/

If you want to read more about other books by this author, they are listed on the following pages...

The Dead Who Do Not Sleep by Jennifer St. Clair

A Beth-Hill Novel (Stand Alone Novels)

Are creatures of the night and all manner of extramundane beings drawn to certain locations in the natural world? In the Midwestern village of Beth-Hill located in southern Ohio, the population is made up of its fair share of common citizens...and much more than its share of supernatural residents. Take a walk on the wild side in this unusual place where imagination meets reality.

Blood of Innocents

Ten years ago, Orien, crown prince of the Seleighe, was captured by his mortal enemies, locked in a dungeon and turned into a vampire. Six years into Orien's sentence, the Healer's brother Cullen disobeyed his mistress's orders to kill him and turned him into a vampire instead, thus sealing both their fates for all eternity.

Now both Orien and Cullen are set free. But a secret only Cullen knows lies locked inside his mind, threatening to drive him mad before he can uncover the identity of a traitor--the very elf who betrayed Orien and left them both to die in darkness.

Publisher: http://www.writers-exchange.com/blood-of-innocents/

Full Moon

Werewolves change into wolves when the moon is full. But Edward's curse only allows him to be *human* when the moon is full.

Alone and despairing, Edward hides himself away from the world. He's scraped out a meager existence for himself for almost a century in the forest he's grown to love and call home. But in the depths of a terrible winter, he stumbles across clues from the life his mother left behind in Faerie. The truth may give him the answers he needs about the source of his birthright... and the curse that holds him captive.

Publisher: http://www.writers-exchange.com/full-moon/

The Dead Who Do Not Sleep by Jennifer St. Clair

A Beth-Hill Novel: Jacob Lane Series

Are creatures of the night and all manner of extramundane beings drawn to certain locations in the natural world? In the Midwestern village of Beth-Hill located in southern Ohio, the population is made up of its fair share of common citizens...and much more than its share of supernatural residents.

Jacob Lane is a ten-year-old girl who's spent her life unaware of her magical heritage. After being sent to Darkbrook, a school of magic, supernatural mysteries seem to spring to life all around her and her new friends.

Book 1: The Tenth Ghost

After Jacob Lane's parents mysteriously vanish, she's sent to Darkbrook, the only school of magic in the United States. While there, she and her new friends stumble upon a series of mysterious deaths in the nine ghosts that haunt the halls of Darkbrook. These ghosts were students who died at the school over the past hundred years. Will Jacob become the tenth ghost, or can she stop a witch's reign of terror?
Publisher: http://www.writers-exchange.com/the-tenth-ghost/

Book 2: The Ninth Guest

When Jacob's friend Ophelia's family decides to open up their castle for guests, amateur paranormal sleuth Jacob Lane is invited to join in on the fun. "Spend the night in a vampire's castle and live to tell the tale!" is supposed to be a fundraiser to help Ophelia's family pay the bills. Heating a castle costs quite a bit, after all. But, after the truth of an old secret is uncovered, what began as an innocent business venture soon turns deadly when vampire hunters get involved.

For years, the vampire hunters have had only one goal: To destroy all vampires. With the help of a new friend, Jacob and Ophelia must work together to save the entire VonBriggle family from extinction.
Publisher: http://www.writers-exchange.com/the-ninth-guest/

Book 3: The Eighth Room

For two hundred years, the Selkies have kept themselves separate from those who live on land. But now the Selkies need allies or they'll be crushed by their ancient enemies, the Finfolk.

Jacob and Ophelia, students at the only school of magic in the United States, uncover a mystery that dates back to Darkbrook's beginnings. While helping clean out old storage rooms for classroom expansion, they find something that might save the Selkies from extinction. With the help of the youngest member of the Wild Hunt who are no longer so wild or terrifying, they must foil the Finfolk who desire the Selkie's destruction...or die trying.

Publisher: http://www.writers-exchange.com/the-eighth-room/

Book 4: The Seventh Secret

After a picture of Niklas, the dragons' liaison to the only school of magic in the United States, shows up in too many newspapers to count, Darkbrook is forced to go on the defensive. The secret of Darkbrook's existence has been discovered. But there are more than dragonhunters in the forest, and, as Jacob Lane, supernatural sleuth and student at Darkbrook, learns how to use her newly discovered talent of healing, she helps to right an old wrong and must battle a teenaged wizard intent on proving--once and for all--that magic is real.

Publisher: http://www.writers-exchange.com/the-seventh-secret/

Book 5: The Sixth Stone

Jacob Lane, supernatural sleuth, and Danny, her werewolf friend, stumble across an alternate world where the Wild Hunt was never bound, and Darkbrook, the school of magic they attend, was abandoned a hundred years ago.

But when the Hounds of the Hunt wish to surrender, the two students are swept up in a whirlwind of heartbreak, betrayal, and the discovery of a lost treasure.

Publisher: http://www.writers-exchange.com/the-sixth-stone/

A Beth-Hill Novella: Karen Montgomery Series

Are creatures of the night and all manner of extramundane beings drawn to certain locations in the natural world? In the Midwestern village of Beth-Hill located in southern Ohio, the population is made up of its fair share of common citizens...and much more than its share of supernatural residents. Take a walk on the wild side in this unusual place where imagination meets reality.

Karen Montgomery was an ordinary woman until she stumbled into the extraordinary... A bargain with elves worth its weight in gold. A plague of sinister ladybugs. Rogue vampire hunters, including one who tries to turn over a new leaf--with disastrous consequences. A ghostly huntsmen of the Wild Hunt wishing for redemption. Karen's life will never be the same again.

Book 1: Budget Cuts

Karen Montgomery is used to taking care of the unpleasant jobs no one else wants to deal with. When a shortage of funds forces her to fire fifteen employees from the library, she isn't happy, but the nasty task has to be done and she is, after all, the boss. But Karen finds finishing her task impossible when she can't seem to track down Ivy Bedinghaus, a night clerk she's never actually met. Once she finally does confront Ivy, she's thrust into a centuries-old conflict that makes her previous troubles radically pale in comparison.
Publisher: http://www.writers-exchange.com/budget-cuts/

Book 2: The Secret of Redemption

Karen Montgomery, librarian, finds herself embroiled in another otherworldly adventure...

A member of the Wild Hunt--ghostly myths that aren't so ghostly (or myth-like) anymore--needs help in reconciling who he once was in life and who he is now.

A little girl has gone missing. And the one most likely responsible for her disappearance is the one Karen must prove innocent.
Publisher: http://www.writers-exchange.com/the-secret-of-redemption/

Book 3: Ladybug, Ladybug

An innocent attempt to rid the library of a plague of ladybugs turns sinister when a rogue vampire hunter gets the contract for pest control.

Ivy Bedinghaus, who works for Karen as a night clerk--along with all the vampires in Beth-Hill--are in danger, and their only hope for survival is with the help of Karen, a member of the Wild Hunt, and Russell Moore, a reformed vampire hunter.

Publisher: http://www.writers-exchange.com/ladybug-ladybug/

Book 4: Detour

One wrong turn sends Karen down a road that shouldn't exist, to the site of an old accident and an even older mystery. With reformed vampire hunter Russell Moore's help, Karen finds the key to the mystery. But Russ keeps his own secrets...some of which are deadly.

When old friends from Russ' past come to call, Karen realizes his secrets might just mean his doom. After a terrible incident three years ago, before Karen met him, Russ wants only to live the rest of his life quietly in Beth-Hill. But his secret might not allow him the new lease on life Russ longs for.

Publisher: http://www.writers-exchange.com/detour/

Companion Story: Russ' Story: Capture

Long before Russell Moore ever met supernatural sleuth Karen Montgomery or set foot in Beth-Hill, he was a vampire hunter, possibly the best vampire hunter of all. He brought down whole nests of vampires, caring little about the consequences of his actions. Anyone who lived with or helped the vampires became enemies to be slaughtered.

So what kind of an idiot would capture a ruthless vampire hunter without a conscience and try to reform him?

Ethan Walker was that idiot. Wanting to protect his family, Ethan set out to prove to Russ that vampires weren't all evil, soulless creatures. If Russ would allow himself to witness their lives, see their humanity, surely he and other vampire hunters like him would let them live in peace. *Surely?*

Publisher: http://www.writers-exchange.com/capture/

Secrets When in Shadow Lie

Twelve years ago, Ryan Grey was cursed by a witch to hide a secret. He's lived with the curse of being unable to die permanently, and, over the years he's slowly losing the memory of his past until almost nothing remains.

But now, after a chance meeting with an elf named Zipporah, he discovers the key to unlocking the secret and breaking the curse once and for all...if he can survive the breaking.

The Dead Who Do Not Sleep

Will Spark only wants a good night's sleep after a night of drinking. Instead, two thugs bang on his door, demanding answers to questions he can't understand. And then they killed him...

Publisher: http://www.writers-exchange.com/the-dead-who-do-not-sleep/

A Beth-Hill Novel: The Abby Duncan Series

Are creatures of the night and all manner of extramundane beings drawn to certain locations in the natural world? In the Midwestern village of Beth-Hill located in southern Ohio, the population is made up of its fair share of common citizens...and much more than its share of supernatural residents. Take a walk on the wild side in this unusual place where imagination meets reality.

Situated in Beth-Hill, where imagination meets reality, is The Rose Emporium, owned by elderly and not-a-little-odd Rose Duncan. The large Victorian house smackdab in the middle of nowhere is a cross between a pawn shop and an antique store that caters to supernatural creatures needing to barter. Rose's twenty-something niece, Abby Duncan, discovers that the world isn't made up of just run-of-the-mill, ordinary humans but an entire spectrum of unusual beings. With her preconceptions about what's normal and what's not turned upside-down, Abby is in for a whole lot of startling truths, mysteries-- about herself and the people and places around her--and danger.

Novella 1: By Any Other Name

Woodturner Abby Duncan decides to sell her spindles at a local Renaissance Festival with only some success. After all, no one really spins their own yarn anymore, do they? While there, she discovers that one of her newfound friends is not what he appears--and his secret is about to get him killed!

Publisher: http://www.writers-exchange.com/by-any-other-name/

Book 2: The Uncrowned Queen

Abby Duncan's elderly Aunt Rose has always been a bit odd. And now she's off on a mysterious trip, leaving Abby behind to run the Rose Emporium, an unusual sort of antique shop. Such an extraordinary store would have been a perfect place for Seth and the others, her friends from the Renaissance Festival, to take a break from traveling between Faires. But when tragedy strikes and Abby and the others discover the true nature of the Rose Emporium, they'll have to travel into Faerie itself before their tightknit group is whole again.

Abby doesn't know much about her family history, but she's about to find out the truth...whether she likes it or not.

Publisher: http://www.writers-exchange.com/the-uncrowned-queen/

Book 3: Coming Soon!

A Beth-Hill Novel: The Shadows Trilogy

Are creatures of the night and all manner of extramundane beings drawn to certain locations in the natural world? In the Midwestern village of Beth-Hill located in southern Ohio, the population is made up of its fair share of common citizens...and much more than its share of supernatural residents. Take a walk on the wild side in this unusual place where imagination meets reality.

A Dreamer dreams the future when the past is not yet laid to rest. Ten years ago, a plague swept across the Seven Kingdoms. Ten years ago, the Queen of Iomar's son was exiled and named the author of the magical plague. Now, in the present, Terrin works to complete his ultimate goal: Control of the Seven Kingdoms using his son's power to supplement his own. But his attempt at dominion meets resistance and the fate of the world rests in the unlikely hands of an exiled prince, a Dreamer, and a vampire...

Book 1: The Prince of Shadows

When Alban's father Terrin appeared at the castle door with a vampire in tow and apologies on his lips, Alban fell under his spell just like everyone else and welcomed him home. But Terrin didn't return to live quietly in his brother's kingdom. He had other plans and, with Alban's untrained powers at his disposal, he begins his ruthless plan to destroy the Seven Kingdoms and rule them all, beginning with his brother's death.

Terrin engineers events to cast the blame on his nephew, Teluride, intending to see the boy executed for his father's murder. But there are those who would thwart Terrin in his mad plan for power, and Alban forms an unlikely alliance with Skade, the reclusive Queen of Iomar, and Terrin's slave, a young vampire with no memory of his name or origins. Although the future looks grim, Alban and the vampire attempt to stop Terrin...and they almost succeed.

A darker history lies at the heart of Terrin's treachery, and only Skade knows the true reason why Terrin would murder his own brother and attempt to destroy both Alban and the vampire to achieve his goals. The Ghost who resides in Skade's mirror--her servant and thrall--holds one of the keys to Terrin's madness. Unfortunately, more than one person wishes for the past to remain the past and the future to hold no shadows of what might have been...

Publisher: http://www.writers-exchange.com/the-prince-of-shadows/

Book 2: Lost In Shadows

Events set in motion ten years ago come to a head as Skade, the reclusive Queen of Iomar, and Nicodemus, who is imprisoned by Skade, struggle to free Alban and the vampire from Terrin's grasp. Old secrets come to light when Skade's exiled son is forced to face his past--or die trying to redeem himself once and for all. Can the crimes of the past truly be forgiven? Only time will tell...and time is running out.

Publisher: http://www.writers-exchange.com/lost-in-shadows/

Book 3: Bound In Shadows

With his power crushed, brother to the king and father to Alban, Terrin is forced to take drastic measures to regain his sons after they are freed and harness the power they possess. But he has an ally inside the healer's house where they are recovering who works to further his plans. The Queen of Iomar, Skade's son, courts redemption to try to save his mother's life, and the vampire who no longer remembers his own name dreams a dream that might save them all...or damn them if success is thwarted.

Publisher: http://www.writers-exchange.com/bound-in-shadows/

A Beth-Hill Novel: Wild Hunt Series

Are creatures of the night and all manner of extramundane beings drawn to certain locations in the natural world? In the Midwestern village of Beth-Hill located in southern Ohio, the population is made up of its fair share of common citizens...and much more than its share of supernatural residents. Take a walk on the wild side in this unusual place where imagination meets reality.

The Wild Hunt roamed the forest outside of Beth-Hill until the Council bound them for a hundred years. Nevertheless, a century of existence has made an indelible mark not easily forgotten for these ghostly myths that are no longer so ghostly or myth-like...

Book 1: Heart's Desire

The Wild Hunt roamed the forest outside of Beth-Hill until the Council bound them for a hundred years--a lifetime for a human but only a passing thought to one such as Gabriel, Master of the Wild Hunt. As the Council's binding draws to a close, old enemies reappear to ensure that the Wild Hunt is bound once more--to a creature much worse than the Council has been.

Publisher: http://www.writers-exchange.com/hearts-desire/

Book 2: Fire and Water

As a young vampire, Erialas Morgan brought his mother back to life with a spell that shouldn't exist, shouldn't have worked...perhaps shouldn't have been performed at all. Desperation and love are his only excuses for doing the unthinkable.

There are others who wish to use that same spell for their own gain--and to destroy the Wild Hunt once and for all. Caught in the middle of a war between the Morgan clan of vampires and their human kin, Erialas turns to the Hunt for help. But even Gabriel, the Master of the Wild Hunt, may not be able to stop the tide of death and destruction once it turns.

Publisher: http://www.writers-exchange.com/fire-and-water/

Book 3: The Lost

Almost sixty years ago, Darkbrook, the only school of magic in the United States, opened its doors to students of decidedly different natures, sending out letters of invitation to the elves, the dragons, and the vampires. The three who responded to the invitation banded together despite their differences but vanished only weeks later along with an entire classroom full of students and their teacher after a field trip gone horribly wrong.

The Wild Hunt has healed and the Hounds have grown closer together, keeping Darkbrook's forest safe and secure for those who live there. Malachi, one of the eldest members of the Wild Hunt, has adapted to Josiah's spell to help him see, but when a demon boy trapped in the body of a human body for sixty years inside the school disrupts the newfound calm, the Hunt--and those they protect--are thrust into a struggle that should have ended long ago when a vampire, an elf, and a dragon vanished into the Mists.

Publisher: http://www.writers-exchange.com/the-lost/

Book 4: A Glint of Silver

Jericho is a vampire who wants is to live away from the Richmond household of vampires led by his ruthless father Connor. When Jericho tries to escape, Connor punishes him and leaves him to die. Tristan is determined to be the one to bring Jericho back, but he can't see him suffer for wanting a normal life. As long as Connor lives, Jericho will never be safe or free. As long as Connor *lives*...

Publisher: http://www.writers-exchange.com/a-glint-of-silver/

Book 5: All That Glitters

As a member of the cruel Morgan Household of vampires, twelve-year-old Arthur Morgan has been abused all his life.

Maya, a water fairy, shows him just how horrible and twisted the household he's grown up is. With her help, and the unexpected help of an adult vampire, Arthur attempts to escape.

Can he become something more than what his father has decreed?

Publisher: http://www.writers-exchange.com/all-that-glitters/

The Chelsea Chronicles

Normally a quiet, serene place, Chelsea Kingdom seems like the perfect location for a centuries' old vampire to blend in and live a normal life, even escape hunters and an angry mob. Unfortunately, his timing couldn't be worse...

Book 1: So You Want to be a Vampire

Chelsea Kingdom is usually a pretty quiet place but recent murders--committed by a vampire--upset the calm. Newcomer to town, Vlad Dhalgren wants only to blend in and live a normal life. He quickly learns that isn't possible, given that other vampires have been hiding in the shadows around the castle--in plain sight--for years.

Despite her lineage, Anna Everett, the crown princess of the Kingdom of Chelsea, isn't a wizard like her father, which means she will never be Queen. She has only one friend, Valerian Moreton--Val--who has secrets he's never shared that could get him *and* Anna killed...

Publisher: http://www.writers-exchange.com/so-you-want-to-be-a-vampire/

Book 2: Transformation

As Anna, crown princess of Chelsea, adjusts to life as a vampire after recent events, Vlad plans for a future he has no real hope to seeing come to pass due to injuries sustained while attempting to save Anna's life. But, as life goes on for Anna and her friend Valerian "Val" Moreton, it changes for others--some of whom are not quite what they seem...

Publisher: http://www.writers-exchange.com/transformation/

You can find ALL our books up on our website at:

http://www.writers-exchange.com

All Jennifer's books:

http://www.writers-exchange.com/Jennifer-St-Clair/

all our fantasy novels:

http://www.writers-exchange.com/category/genres/fantasy/

Milton Keynes UK
Ingram Content Group UK Ltd.
UKHW020119030823
426203UK00016B/722